NOTHING HERE IS REAL

A Novel

Matt Bindig

NFB
Buffalo, New York

Cover design by Diane Bond
Cover Painting *Woods I* by Laura Wilder

NFB
<<<>>>
No Frills Buffalo/Amelia Press
119 Dorchester Road
Buffalo, New York 14213

For more information visit
nofrillsbuffalo.com

*For Theresa with love,
and my children with gratitude.*

NOTHING HERE IS REAL

"...How foolish it is to long for childhood,
to want to run in circles in the yard again,
arms outstretched,
pretending to be an airplane.

How senseless to dread whatever lies before us
when, night and day, the boats,
strong as horses in the wind,
come and go,

bringing in the tiny infants
and carrying away the bodies of the dead."

Billy Collins

RETURN

The lingering clouds colored the sky with smudges of inky darkness. Even though it was morning, the antique streetlights of Apollo, New York, so carefully preserved by the historical society, still burned behind the sturdy trees that lined the length of Water Street. Their light, filtered by the dewy branches, caused shadows to fall in dappled splash patterns across the damp road, and gave Grady Pickett the disquieting impression that dusk was falling at dawn.

Here was the town he knew as a boy. The houses of his classmates were all the same except for maybe a fresh coat of paint or a new deck wrapped around the front door. The Methodist church, where he sat each Sunday, squeezed next to his brother Emile, stood stone silent, as it always had, on the corner of Gendel and Water Street. The familiar stores where he spent his allowance on baseball cards and Christmas presents were closed. It was just shy of 5:00 a.m.

Grady looked over at the tawny envelope that, along with the small wooden box that was everything to him now, had ridden shotgun all the way from Massachusetts. For the seventh time since he'd crossed back into New York, he pulled out the article his father had sent him announcing the opening of The Red Newt Art Gallery, whose first show would feature Ward Gregory's three previously lost paintings. The sedan's engine still hummed. Grady's foot still pressed the brake firmly to the ground.

Ward Gregory. Seeing the name there, illuminated by his hometown's streetlights, caused Grady's mind to flash with a series of indelible images: the toilet full of blood, the knife tumbling across the kitchen floor, his brother on his knees in the middle of a field of snow, and the beds of his own boyish fingernails, raw from his effort to scrub away the evidence of his crime. He slid the car into park and shut it off.

The first signs of life were now beginning to stir outside the storefronts. Grady tucked the box under his arm and, leaving all that was left of his belongings packed in the car behind him, walked away toward Worthingdale Woods without looking back.

THE ARTIST

All I knew of the old man who lived across the street in the house with the big fence around his yard was that he wore a gray wool three-piece suit, usually with a pastel tie, and handed my father the gold offering plate each Sunday. If my parents' knew anything else about him, they didn't let on.

Two weeks before I was to turn twelve, the cold-snap that had been gripping all of Western New York since the middle of December broke and the weather turned unseasonably warm. A few days later the highs were in the mid-forties and the snow that had been

accumulating in the region since just
before Thanksgiving began to peel away
in massive layers from the corner drifts.

Rain was coming down in half-
frozen sheets when Ward Gregory rang our
doorbell for the first time. My father
invited him in.

"How can I help you, Mr. Gregory?"

"Well, I didn't know if you folks
wanted to take a walk down to see the big
cave-in?"

"I'm not sure what you mean."

"With all the run off, and now
with the rain, the ice dams in Shenengo
Creek gave loose and what with the water
running so high and all, Water Street
just gave way."

"You're telling me Water Street
collapsed?" my father asked.

"That I am, Frank."

"Well, thanks for the news, Ward,
but I think Marty and I will keep
the boys in tonight. Wouldn't want 'em
catching colds."

"They will anyway-they always do-but suit yourself." He smiled, turned and walked down our front path and out the end of the driveway without any further acknowledgement of my dad.

Three months later I found a crumpled flyer with no postage in our mailbox announcing the opening of a show at the Albright Knox Art Gallery in Buffalo. It proclaimed:

Ward Gregory's Triumphant Return to the Buffalo Art Scene:

Shenengo Falls - A Series of Landscapes in Oil

Exclusive opening showing April 22, 1987 - 7:00-9:30 p.m.

Scribbled below in his own shaky hand was the note: *I'd love to see all of you there. Ward.* I showed it to Emile when he came home from school, and he took it hastily up to his room and closed the door behind him.

When he produced the note at dinner that evening and passed it over to my father, my dad read it over, then looked up quizzically at my mother. "Ward's an artist?"

"Let me see that." She read it

silently.

"You knew that Frank. They told us when we bought the house."

"I guess it never occurred to me that they were serious. I guess I thought they were just trying to say that it was a nice area... is a nice area." He corrected himself.

"That's next Friday. Can we go, Mom?"

"Emile, you know very well that next Friday is Good Friday. I'm not sure how I feel about us going to an art show on the night that Jesus died."

"I don't see the big deal, Marty. If the kids want to go, why shouldn't we let them? Besides, it'll give you a reason to get dressed up."

"Yeah, Mom," Emile said. "And besides, I think Mr. Gregory seems like an interesting guy. I've always thought there's got to be something going on behind that fence--you know, something cool."

"That's what worries me," my mother

said. She turned to face me. "Do you want
to go, Grady?"

"Sure, I like paintings."

"Okay," she said. "We'll go."

None of us spoke on the way home
from the show. Though we had seen a
miraculous thing, the experience felt
beyond words. As we shuffled inside the
house, my father broke the silence.

"That was something, huh?"

"I've never seen pictures like that
before," Emile said in a whisper. "The way
he painted them... it kind of looked like
everything was still happening."

The show consisted of three
paintings depicting the same spot on the
Shenengo Creek from different vantage
points.

The first showed the rising water
in shades of purple and gray through
the eyes of someone being pulled toward
the mouth of the Water Street tunnel as
it had stood before its recent collapse.
There was something breathless in the

way the paint splashed at the edges of the canvas. Something that made you yearn for light and air, to be free of the swelling waters.

A collection of black walnut trees was clustered around the entrance to the tunnel (or had been until the structure collapsed, bringing the trees down with it). These trees had long been a source of contention in town. Every fall they dropped an ungodly number of melting green nuts that would rot, stink, and stain the street and shoes of the passing pedestrians. Ward Gregory had painted his second portrait from the vantage point of one nestled in the branches of one of these trees. One could hardly make out the swirling creek through the broad strokes he used to represent the limbs. It was almost as if the water wasn't there.

The third portrait was of two boys. The left hand of the boy still clinging to the bank was wrapped tightly around an exposed root of a nearby sapling. His face was a mask of pain and fear so

convincingly wrought that the hairs on
the back of my neck stood up as I stared
at it. His right hand was extended
to the other boy in the picture, whose
body was almost totally submerged in
the ice-chunked water. The drowning
boy's desperate hand stretched out
of the creek's ice and snow. The only
visible water was the rushing flow that
surrounded his half-open mouth. Anyone
who saw the painting knew his struggle
against the currents of the icy stream
was doomed to be futile.

As the four of us gazed, slack-
jawed, at the third painting, I felt a
foreign hand fall on my shoulder. Ward
Gregory stood between my brother and me.

"I'm glad you came tonight," he
whispered to us. "I'm glad you got to see
this now, before you're older."

"It's quite a show, Ward," my
father interrupted, reaching for Ward
Gregory's right hand, which was resting
on the small of my brother's back.
Gregory released my shoulder and shook

my father's left hand awkwardly. Then
he straightened himself and smiled.
"Thanks, Frank. I trust that you found
the place okay."

"Oh, Grady had a field trip here
last year. I took the day off to chaperone
it. I'm one of those landmark guys when
it comes to directions. You drive me
someplace once, and I'll never forget how
to get there."

"That's a nice skill to have," Ward
Gregory smiled. "I guess I still get lost
every once in while, even in Apollo."

"Well, I don't see how that could
happen. Marty tells me you've lived there
all your life."

"Only if you measure it in years,"
the artist said. Then quickly he added,
"Listen, as charming as this has been,
I do need to attend to my other guests.
Thanks so much for coming, boys. Marty."
As he walked away I realized two things.
First, it wasn't until Ward Gregory
acknowledged my mother that she released
her breath and looked away from the

last painting, wiping away the tears of
recognition gathered on her face. Second,
it wasn't until he walked away that Ward
Gregory removed his hand from the small
of my brother's back.

That spring Ward Gregory tore
down his privacy fence. It took him all
three days of Memorial Day weekend. He
did it with a four-pound hammer and a
spade. Working from the inside out, he
would hit the upper part of the boards
of the fence until their nails came loose
from the crossties. Then he would bend
over and repeat this step with the lower
part, until the board splintered free
from the fence and a gap would open up
in the previously uninterrupted wall of
seclusion.

When all of the boards and
crossties were down, he set about digging
up the posts, each of which was set in
a blob of concrete four feet below the
surface of the soil. It was a display of
diligence, if not efficiency. But what I

remember most about that weekend, while
I watched in wonder from the shade of
our backyard, was the man's appearance.
He hammered and sweat in a pair of khaki
pants, a white linen oxford shirt with
a silk maroon tie, and deep burgundy
penny-loafers. Each of the three days
he emerged from the house in the same
clothes, freshly laundered and pressed
with starched creases visible from forty
yards away.

   The next Saturday I awoke at 7:00
a.m. to the sound of a lawn mower. When I
opened the curtains of my bedroom window,
I was stunned to see Ward Gregory atop
a riding lawn mower dressed in the same
gray wool suit he wore to church and a
blue construction hard hat, his brow
furrowed with concentration as he drove
the mower in diagonal lines across his
very walkable lawn.

   As I watched the old man from my
window, a small, squatty figure dressed
in faded boxer shorts, a ripped T-shirt,
and bedroom slippers stomped across the

freshly mowed grass and stood directly
in the path of the machine. It took a few
beats for me to realize the small, apple-
shaped man frantically motioning at Ward
Gregory in a red-faced display of anger
was Frank C. Pickett, my father, the
pacifist.

From what I could tell, they
were exchanging words, although Ward
Gregory's back was to me. His hands were
moving, and more than once he took a step
toward my father, only to have my father
back away. After five minutes both men
shook hands and proceeded to push the
riding mower, in neutral, back into the
garage, leaving the lawn half-finished.

The curious incident drove me from
my room. I met my father in the kitchen,
trying my best to act as though I had no
idea why he was walking in from outside
at half-past seven in the morning,
wearing the clothes he had slept in.

Before I could say anything,
my father deadpanned, "See anything
interesting out your window this

morning?"

"How did you know?"

"I didn't. That psycho Ward Gregory, who by the way told me he was wearing a hard-hat just in case a branch from one of his trees happened to fall as he was riding under it, told me that you had been watching him for twenty minutes."

"That's not true," I said. My father looked directly in my eyes. "I was only watching him for about half that time. How did he know that, anyway?"

"I have no idea. All I know is that when I told him that either of my boys would gladly mow his lawn for him at a reasonable time of day, he pointed out that if that was the case, why hadn't you scampered over to offer, given the fact that you had been watching him for a half of an hour."

"I wasn't watching him for that long."

"Anyway, the only way I could get the loony to stop mowing his lawn at 7:00 a.m. on a Saturday was to agree to have you or Emile finish mowing it for him this afternoon. What do you say? Do you want first dibs?"

"What'll he pay me?"

"I have no idea, but whatever it is, it's more than your brother will make today."

"Okay, what do I have to do?"

"Just go over there after lunch," my father said. "I'll lend you a tie."

I arrived across the street in shorts and a T-shirt at 12:35 p.m.. Ward Gregory's door had a knocker on it fashioned to look like a woodpecker. A string extended from the woodpecker's tail, and when it was pulled, the beak of the bird rapped a metal plate that was placed in the center of the door. After three raps, Mr. Gregory's face appeared in one of the small glass windowpanes at the top of the door, and he spoke to me without opening it.

"Your father said you would arrive after lunch."

"We just finished eating."

"I was expecting your brother. Is he not available today? I asked for him."

"No," I said flatly. As I stood talking to the old man through the closed door, I began to feel peculiar. Why wasn't he opening the door? "Listen, Mr. Gregory, I can mow your lawn now. Or do you want me to come back tomorrow?"

"No, now would be fine, Grady. There's a push mower in the garage that's all gassed up for the occasion. I assume a young boy like you won't mind walking the fields."

"I'll be all right."

"And, Grady, one more thing. I'm sorry to be so rude and speak to you through the door. I'm afraid you caught me by surprise with your early arrival, and I'm not halfway decent. Stop back when you're done mowing, and we'll have a chat. Do you like lemonade?"

"Yeah, I drink that."

"Good. Now be sure to stick to the pattern I've established on the grass.

I've got an artistic reputation to uphold,
you know."

I finished the lawn in less than
half an hour, and when I knocked on
the door again, Mr. Gregory answered
it wearing broad-legged linen pants, a
faintly yellow silk shirt unbuttoned to
just above the navel, and nothing on his
feet.

"Come in, my boy. I'm just getting
dressed."

I followed him in and was happy to
see that while he walked from the door to
the kitchen he buttoned up his shirt.

"You're uneasy, Grady. Is there
something wrong?"

"No, Mr. Gregory. I'm just pretty
sweaty, and your house is so nice. I don't
want to ruin anything."

"Not at all. Have a seat." I sat in
a tall chair next to a wrought-iron cafe
table with a wicker top covered in glass.
He handed me a glass of lemonade. "Drink
up," he said, and he downed his glass in
one quick motion. "You don't mind if I mix

myself another, do you?"

"No, that's okay," I said.

He stood with his back to me and
fixed himself a drink out of two bottles,
then turned back to me with a tumbler
full of tinkling liquid in his hand.
"You know, my boy, that angry father of
yours gave me a great idea this morning.
Would you like to make this mowing job a
regular thing?"

"Uh... that's tough to say, Mr.
Gregory. I've got baseball a lot in the
summer and . . ."

"Ah, baseball. What is it about that
game that causes so many good men to lose
their minds?"

"I'm not sure what you mean, sir?"

"My father loved the game. He even
coached a little league team for a while,
but they said he didn't know what he was
doing. Of course, it wasn't true. He was a
fine coach, but the team wasn't winning,
and another father wanted a try. Still,
it hurt my father's feelings, what they
said about him. He was a very sensitive

man, one who cared deeply about what others thought of him. I never understood that. The way I see it, if you can see the truth of your own life, what does it matter if everyone else can only sees lies? Does that make sense to you?"

"I guess. I mean sort of, I think."

"Anyway, if you're not up to the job, do you imagine that Emile would be interested?"

"Well, sir..."

"Grady, you can call me 'Ward.' Calling me 'sir' makes me nervous."

"Okay, I... I guess I really couldn't speak for Emile. He kind of does his own thing now."

"Yes, he does his own thing, and you do baseball."

"It's not like that, sir..."

"Grady, we've been over this."

"Right, it's not like that. It's just that I really couldn't speak for him is all."

"You've grown up a lot this year, haven't you? I mean, you're quite a young man now, aren't you?"

"I don't know."

"My God, when I was your age I had no idea my father would be dead in less than five years." The smile was gone from his face. I was silent.

"Would you like a tour of the house before you go? I'm sure you've been dying to see all the bedrooms."

"You know, Mr. Gregory . . ."

He stood up so quickly that the table shook, and I had to scramble to keep my still-full glass of lemonade from tumbling to the floor.

"Damn it, boy. You're trying my patience." Then smiling again, "It's Ward."

"Okay," I said. "Actually, I better go."

"I think so too," he said through the bottom of his second glass. I walked out of the house, while he remained seated in the chair.

"I'll let Emile know about the job," I said over my shoulder.

"Do that."

My hands were shaking as I closed the door behind me. It wasn't until I got home that I realized I'd mowed his lawn for free.

When I told Emile about the possibility of mowing Ward Gregory's lawn, he smiled at me and said, "What, did you let him scare you or something?"

"I'm not scared of him," I said.

"How's the pay?"

"Good enough," I said. Let him go mow the damn lawn for free and find out for himself, I thought.

"Obviously not, if you're giving the job to me."

"Look Emile, the job's yours if you want it. I've got baseball on Saturdays."

"You and your baseball," my brother laughed.

The next Saturday as Ricky Dominski and his father were picking me up for my afternoon little league game, my brother headed off to mow Ward

Gregory's lawn. As we drove home later
that afternoon, I was giddy with the
anticipation of hearing about what I was
sure would be Emile's embarrassment at
being snubbed by our neighbor, but to my
great disappointment, when I walked in
the door, my brother was nowhere to be
found.

"Where's Emile, Mom? I want to talk
to him about something important."

"I haven't seen him since late this
morning. I'm sure he'll show up soon."

But Emile didn't show up until
dinner was being served. My mother had
been pacing with worry for an hour at
that point and embraced him with an
awkward hug the second he walked in the
door. "Where have you been?"

"I was mowing Mr. Gregory's lawn.
Then I was just hanging out in the
woods."

"Next time a call would be nice.
Your mother's been out of her mind ever
since your brother came home," my father
chided.

"I'd be worried too. All that kid
does is play baseball."

"Screw you, Emile," I shot back.

"That is no way to talk to your
brother," my mother scolded.

"But he was saying that to me. Why
am I getting yelled at when Emile is the
one who's in trouble?"

"Who do you think you are, talking
back to me like that?"

"Mom."

"You get the hell to your room, you
hear me?"

"But all I said was . . ."

"I don't care. If you think for one
second you can talk to me that way, you've
got another thing coming, little man."

"Fine." I slunk to my room and
slammed the door behind me.

Forty minutes later, as I was lying
on my bed looking up at the ceiling, my
bedroom door opened without a knock, and
to my great surprise, Emile walked in. He
sat down next to me.

"I snuck you a roll. I figured you

might be hungry."

I said nothing, but took it thankfully. After I had finished chewing, I looked up to find my brother was crying.

"What are you crying about?" I asked.

He wiped the tears off of his face, grabbed me by the shoulders, and pulled me into a sitting position. "I've got to tell you something, but you have to swear that no matter what, you'll never tell anyone, not even Mom and Dad."

Although Emile and I were close in age, we had never really been the type of brothers to share intimacies. Even as a young child I knew that he included me in his schemes more out of obligation than genuine affection, and often only after some heavy-handed prodding from my parents who had always wished that there was more of a kinship between their two boys. Still, from time to time he would soften his stance toward me, and experience taught me not to question his

kindness or shrink too forcefully from
his sometimes violent mood swings, for to
do so would certainly lead to a widening
of the chasm between us, a chasm I had
always been desperate to make disappear.

"Okay, I promise I won't tell
anyone," I said.

Emile sat back and gathered
himself before he continued. When he
was sure I was hanging on his words, he
said, "Today I went to mow Ward's lawn." I
nodded. "Well, first he took me into the
garage to show me how to work the push
lawn mower. I told him I already knew
how to do it, but he insisted on showing
me the damn thing, walking me through
every step of working it. When I was done
mowing the lawn, he invited me in for
lemonade."

"He did the same thing to me."

Emile's eyes were wide with worry.
"What happened next, Grady? You've got to
tell me."

"Nothing, I just left and came
home."

Nothing Here is Real

"Well, after I drank a few glasses
of lemonade, he told me he thought I had
it in me to be a real artist. He told me
that if I wanted to, he could show me how
to get started. He asked me if I wanted
to see some of his work. Some stuff that
nobody had ever seen before." All the
time Emile was talking he was looking
straight into the mirror I had hung
on the wall above my dresser; you could
see it from my bed if you sat up really
straight.

"So what, did he show you some
paintings or something?" My heart felt
tight in my chest, and I wasn't sure
why.

"He took me on a tour of his house.
We went in all these rooms and on every
wall were these crazy paintings. You've
never seen anything like it. He took me
over to this one painting in his bedroom
that was all crazy colors and numbers
all mixed together. He told me that if
I looked at it long enough, I would see
my own true reflection. Then he told me

he would be right back. A few minutes
later he said, 'Emile,' and when I turned
around he was on all fours on his bed
with his pants around his ankles."

"Jesus."

"He had a bottle of ointment in
his hand. He was talking in this weird
voice that sounded like an old woman
crying. He told me that if I would rub
the ointment between his cheeks while
holding on to him with my other hand
that he would give me thirty dollars."

"That sick bastard." Emile was as
white as a sheet. "What did you do? Tell
me you slapped him or something."

"I couldn't do anything like that.
The guy had me trapped in his room."

"He's old. You could have kicked his
ass."

"It wasn't like that, Grady. I can't
really explain it. I know this sounds
crazy, but I almost felt like if I had
reacted that way, I don't know, it's
like I would have hurt his feelings or
something."

"Who cares?" I shouted. "Jesus, Emile you're not telling me you did it, are you? Tell me you didn't do it."

"No, I just told him that I couldn't. That I liked girls, not guys. That's what I said."

"And what did he do?"

"He just got up, pulled his pants up really slow. He didn't even turn around. Then he said, 'Okay,' and walked out of the room."

"That's it?"

"That's it."

"Then what did you do?"

"I came home. What do you think?'

"Emile, we've got to tell Mom and Dad. . ."

"Listen, Grady. You swore to me you wouldn't tell a soul. You swore it. If you go back on your word, I'll kill you. I swear to God!"

"What? Why?"

"Ward's not a bad guy. He's just a sad old man, who's lonely. You don't know him like I do is all I'm saying."

"What does that mean? You've only been over there once."

"You don't know everything about me, Grady." He looked away and then added, "And besides, if you tell Mom and Dad, they'll just go squawking to the cops, and he'll end up in jail."

"Which is where he belongs."

Emile was almost desperate now. "Grady, listen. I promise I'll never go over there again. But you've got to swear that you'll never say anything about this to anyone. No one. Got it?"

"I don't know, Emile. This doesn't seem right."

"Look, it's all right. I promise, okay."

"You didn't like it, did you? I mean seeing him like that."

"No, I didn't like it, and besides, I didn't do anything. I'm not like that. I've got a girl right now, Mary Fussell, that I'm close to hooking up with."

The fact that my brother was now talking openly to me about his love life

was almost as shocking to me as the fact
that he had had a close encounter with
a sexual predator just that afternoon.
"Yeah right," I said awkwardly.

"The only thing that's holding me
back is that I never get any practice."

"What do you mean?"

"I mean, I've never really kissed
a girl or anything like that, so I don't
really know what I'm doing. Guys are
supposed to know what they're doing.
Girls can tell if you don't. They only
want to be with guys who know."

"How do you know all this anyway?"
I asked.

"You just know when you get older,
Grady. You just know."

He let those words hang in the
silence between us as we sat together on
the edge of my bed. Then Emile pulled me
into a hug.

Not since we were young boys had
he willingly hugged me. I was stiff and
silent. My neck was wet with his breath.
I lifted my arms up to hug him back, but

he pulled away from my embrace, looked
straight into my eyes, and kissed me
flush on the mouth.

I screamed and broke free, spitting
his taste from my lips.

"Calm down, Grady. I've got to
practice is all. Girls know when you don't
know what you're doing." His voice was
shaking and his eyes were brimming with
tears.

"Yeah, well practice on someone else.
I'm not a fag." Before the last syllable
was out of my mouth, his fist smashed
into my jaw. I fell back on the bed. His
knees were on my chest, his hands held
onto both of my wrists.

"You done?" he said, blinking away
the tears that pooled in his eyes.

"Get off of me!" I was the one crying
now. "I'm telling Mom and Dad." Then his
hand went to my throat. I strained to
breathe, but no air would come.

"You can't breathe now, can you?"
he asked. I blinked my eyes in response.
"Well, you say one word of what just

happened, and you're dead. You got me?
Dead." He let go of my throat.

"Fine," I coughed. "Now, get off me."

"Oh, I will." He released my left
wrist and let fall a straight blow to my
mouth followed by a sharp hook to the
side of my face.

My lips split, and I instantly
tasted my own blood. I rolled toward my
pillow and buried my face in its downy
banks. My breaths were coming short and
fast; by the time one was halfway out, I
was gasping to get another in. I rolled
out of the pillow and onto my back. My
eyes closed, and I began to spin in a free
fall. Sky and tree branches washed before
me. I felt the dam breaking and the icy
chill of water washing over me. I looked
for my brother; I reached for his hand,
but all I saw was the closing door. And
then with a slam, he was gone.

I awoke in the middle of the night.
Whoever had come into my room to turn
off the light and pull the covers over my

sleeping body failed to notice the blood
that had gathered on my pillow. My lips
felt dry. I pulled myself up in stages. A
woozy humming sound in my head greeted
me when I stood to examine the shadow
that looked back at me from the mirror
above my dresser. My curtains were open,
but the night sky gave me no light by
which to assess the damage Emile's fists
had done to my face. My parents' bedroom
was down the hallway; I had no idea what
time it was but didn't dare turn on the
light, lest they notice that I was awake
and begin to ask questions I'd have no
idea how to answer. After letting my eyes
adjust to the dark, I realized the hall
light, which usually shone under my door
when my parents were awake, was out.
Everyone was asleep.

I opened my bedroom door and crept
past Emile's room and into the bathroom.
I turned on the light. The three-fold
mirror reflected a horror show of blood
and bruising. After Emile had left the
room, I had rolled onto my left side,

facing the wall. The blood from my split
lips had dribbled down that side of
my face and coagulated in a brown and
bumpy mass that gave me the look of a
bearded man who had been called away
midway through stripping himself of his
facial disguise. Augmenting the effects
of the dried blood was a purplish rose of
a bruise that was beginning to bloom in
front of my left ear, where Emile's second
blow landed. How would I explain this to
my parents?

I soaped up my hands and washed
the side of my face. I blinked back the
tears of pain as my lips burned with the
water; both the upper and lower lips were
split. I turned off the water, dried my
face and then, without much thought,
emptied my bladder into the waiting bowl.

As I went to flush, I was stunned
to see the water in the toilet was full
of blood. Instantly and fully awake, my
first reaction was to grab myself to see
if the blood was my own.

It wasn't my blood. Someone else in

my family had bled out into the toilet
and either wasn't aware of it or had left
the evidence in the hope that the mess
would be discovered. I closed the lid and
pulled the lever to wash away the stains.
By the time the water rose again, it
looked as if nothing had happened.

I turned off the light and crept
back down the hall toward Emile's room.
I was relieved to find his door slightly
ajar. I slipped past the doorknob
and waited for my eyes to embrace the
darkness of the room.

My brother still slept with one
naked, recycled Christmas tree light
plugged into the socket next to his bed.
His head was turned toward the door and
his mouth was a gradually widening hole
through which the heavy breaths of sleep
escaped in rhythmic wheezes. His hair was
an auburn mess of snarls that fell across
his smooth forehead. As I stood next to
him there, staring down at his innocent,
sleeping face, the rage I had felt toward
him earlier seeped out of my heart, and

Nothing Here is Real

I was slapped with an image of the past
so palpable I staggered backwards to the
foot of his bed to escape it.

It was one of my first years of
school. All of the students were milling
around the outside of the main entrance
of the building, dawdling over getting
onto the buses to be taken home. Even
though Emile was older than I was, we
were released from school at the same
time each day. We usually walked home
together, but for some reason that year,
my parents signed Emile up for an after-
school floor hockey league at the high
school, which meant that on Mondays,
Wednesdays and Thursdays, he would take
the bus with the other aspiring pucksters
to the high school gymnasium for league
play.

What my parents must not have
known is that Emile, who by virtue of the
fact that he was stubbornly outspoken
and constantly insisted on having his
own way in any game he played, was

relentlessly abused by his classmates. This, plus the fact Emile made no secret of hating hockey (just as he hated almost every other sport) all but assured that those who played it, hated Emile back with equal vigor.

Emile was usually able to escape after-school bullying by slipping out of the side door to walk home with me, but things changed once hockey started. Before the snow began to gather in earnest, he was simply subjected to taunting insults from his cooler peers and the occasional cuff on the shoulder or the side of the head when he was stupid enough to try to defend himself against their verbal onslaught, but when there was snow enough to throw, things really got bad for him.

My best guess now is that the teachers who gathered in the doorways to "supervise" the children as they boarded the buses resented this duty, and as a sign of defiance, decided to look the other way as the snowballs flew

through the air, pelting unsuspecting
kindergarteners and fearless fifth-
graders with equal accuracy and velocity.
If they had cared to pay attention, they
would have seen an inordinate number of
those snowballs hurled in my brother's
direction. Even the heavily bundled
students in the lower grades caught on
and took to waiting behind the piles
of snow on either side of the doorway,
or hiding behind one of the naked oak
trees that spotted the school's side lawn,
in anticipation of my brother's exiting
the building and making his hurried
passage to the bus. Every day he faced
a hailstorm of objects that ranged in
consistency from spheres of packed powder
to globs of stinging, slushy mess. Despite
the fact that arm accuracy is typically
one of the last athletic skills to develop
in growing boys, seldom were the days my
brother made it from the door to the bus
unscathed.

      My reaction the first time I saw
the assault my brother endured was

to run to his defense, or at the very
least to let the long-coats who stood
supervising the chaos know that his life
was in danger. In fact, I did as much
and more in my mind each day as I walked
home alone, mentally playing out scenes
of heroic rescues or cinematic scenarios
where my brother and I stood back-to-back,
taking on all comers. But the simple,
and to me shameful, truth was that I did
nothing. I too occupied a low position in
the school's social hierarchy, and I knew,
even at a young age, that to rush to my
brother's defense, or to even acknowledge
the fact that "that kid, Emile" and I
shared the same last name ensured that
I too would suffer Emile's social fate.
So, instead, I watched from the doorway,
unseen by the outside observers, as the
snowballs flew. Only when the bus doors
folded shut would I expose myself to the
elements and embark upon my solitary
walk home.

It was my brother's former teacher
Mrs. Hessey who forced the moment to its

crisis. One Thursday afternoon, I stood
huddled behind the crash bar, watching
as Emile suffered a particularly brutal
attack. He sprinted for his bus, only to
be tripped by a fourth-grade girl. He
fell, face-first, into the salt-induced
slush of the sidewalk. His backpack lay
sprawling and open in the snow. As he
picked himself up to gather his things,
a classmate kicked his math book into
a nearby snowdrift, and another came
along and picked up his pencil case
and skipped it, never to be seen again,
underneath an idling bus. Upon seeing
the pencil case, which he had negotiated
heavily for at the beginning of the school
year, go skipping across the slush like
a stone across the smooth surface of a
creek, Emile seemed to decide to let the
desecration be complete before he began to
try to gather his things again. He stood,
dumbly, with a hangdog look of shame on
his face and waited for the next kick to
come.

Just in that moment Mrs. Hessey

came up behind me where I stood at my
solitary outpost, put both of her hands
on my shoulders, and with her hip,
pushed open the school door. In a voice
loud enough to be heard over the roar of
the buses and screeching of the children,
she cried, "That's your brother out there,
Pickett. Go help him out."

I turned toward her in horror as
she pushed me out the door and let it
close solidly behind her. My coat was
unzipped. My scarf hung loose around
my neck. My gloves were gathered in one
hand. My hat was in the other. Emile
turned toward the door and stared at me
a full beat before a snowball crashed
into the side of his head. The force of
the impact spun him toward the buses.
He didn't look back. He simply bent over,
picked up the things around his feet,
and walked toward his bus. I could see
from where I stood that the slush from
the initial hit was running down his
coat collar, but he made no attempt to
wipe it away nor to dodge the other

objects flying at him, which regularly
struck his back, legs, and finally again
the back of his head before he was able
to climb safely onto the bus that would
transport him to the high school. It was
only after he sat down in the front seat
and slid all the way over to the window
that he lifted his eyes to meet mine
again.

In his look of resignation, I
could see he had known all along that I
watched his daily torture. He knew, and
he wanted to be sure I knew as well.

I ran across the small snowfield
that separated the parking lot from the
school's side door. "Emile, Emile, wait."

But he never blinked, not even as a
boy who just climbed onto the bus pushed
his face against the window. His hat was
jerked off his head as the boy pulled
it free, along with a fistful of Emile's
hair; then the boy ran to the back of the
bus, leaving Emile stunned and silent.
The boy opened the bus's back window and
threw Emile's hat out onto the waiting

snow. I stopped short on the sidewalk
next to the bus, looking up at my brother.
His eyes never left mine as the bus
pulled away.

I waited until all of the buses were
gone before I gathered up my brother's
hat and what I could find of the rest of
his things in the scattered snow.

I cried as I walked home that day.
When I got home I avoided my mother and
went directly to Emile's room. Not knowing
what to do or say, I cleaned off the snow
and slush from his belongings and piled
them neatly on the corner of his desk.

That evening, after he complained
of an upset stomach, Emile was allowed
to skip dinner. He didn't go to school the
next day either. My mother prevented me
from going in to see him under the guise
that she "didn't want me to catch the
bug." When he did return to school in the
middle of the next week, the floor hockey
season was over.

"What are you doing in here?"

Emile sat up in his bed and was speaking to me in a hushed, angry tone.

When I said, "I didn't want to wake you up," his demeanor softened.

"Well, the next time you don't want to wake someone up, I suggest you don't go into their room in the middle of the night and stand at the end of their bed staring at them. You're getting weirder by the minute, you know." There was a kidding kindness in his words that took me by surprise.

"Did you have a bad dream or something?" He spoke to me as if we were both much younger--as if the events from earlier in the evening hadn't happened. I reached up and touched my lip to be sure. It was still throbbing.

"Emile, listen. I was just in the bathroom. The toilet was full of blood. I think I want to tell Mom and Dad."

He was silent. His gasps came first; then he put his hand over his face and began to sob. "Grady, I'm so scared. I don't know what to do."

"It's okay," I said. "Mom and Dad will know."

"I'm just a fucked up pussy. Everybody is right about me."

"No, Emile, it's not like that. You've just got to tell Mom and Dad."

"Why did it have to be this way?" I was sure our folks could hear us.

"I don't know, Emile, but you've got to promise me you'll tell them."

He buried his face in his blankets. His whole body shook from his cries. I sat on the edge of the bed. "You've got to promise me you'll tell them... then everything will be okay. Promise me." Slowly he stopped crying and lay silently without moving.

"Promise me that you'll tell them, Emile. I don't want to do it."

He sat up and wiped the tears and snot from his face. He looked at me in the darkness, lay back down, covered himself with the blankets, and turning toward the wall said, "I promise."

"Good. Will you do it, tomorrow?"

"I don't know when I'll do it, but I promise I will."

"Okay, Emile. I'm going to bed now. No hard feelings, though, huh?"

"No way."

I walked across the room silently. When I reached the door, my brother spoke again, louder than before. "Hey, Grady?"

"Yeah?"

"Will you stay in here until I fall asleep?"

I walked back over to his bed without saying a word and sat down with my back against his nightstand looking away from Emile. A few minutes later he was breathing heavily.

At dinner the next night we ate to the sounds of silverware against plates, muffled gulps, and the shuffling of dishes. We finished eating quickly, and as my brother rose to excuse himself to his room, I spoke up. "Mom," I said. "Did Mr. Gregory call here today?"

"No, he didn't. Why do you ask?"

"Well, I just know that he and

Emile... that next week Emile is supposed to mow his lawn." I was speaking to my mother, but my eyes were on my brother.

"I'm not sure what the arrangement is, Grady."

"I'm on it," Emile said flatly.

"What does that mean?" I asked.

"It means, mind your own business. Understand?"

"Look," my mother interjected, "if you boys are arguing over who gets to mow the lawn, you'll just have to work it out yourselves, okay?"

"That's not it Mom," I said. "I just think that maybe . . ."

"Why don't you just shut your mouth, Grady?" Emile snapped.

"What is going on here? Can't we just eat our dinner in peace?" my mother asked sharply.

I stood up. "Either you say it or I will, Emile."

Emile looked at me and smiled out of the corner of his mouth. "Okay," he said.

Nothing Here is Real

"May I be excused?" I asked.

"If it means I can eat one meal this week in peace, then yes," my mother said. I picked up my dishes, carried them into the kitchen, and was out the front door before Emile began speaking.

When I returned to the house, I found the dishes still on the dinner table and full of half-eaten scraps. The chairs were askew. My father's paper napkin lay on top of his plate. The only thing missing was my family. It was as if they had been lifted from the table mid-bite.

As I made my way down the hallway toward the bedrooms, I heard my mother's voice, loud and foreign, from behind her door. My father stood outside their room with his hand against the top of the door. He looked as though he were leaning against a tree that was destined to collapse-the look on his face reflected his belief that as long as he kept on leaning, the tree would not fall.

"Marty, we've got to think this

through before we do anything."

My mother did not speak in
response. The only reply was the crashing
of unseen objects against the walls of
their bedroom.

"Marty, open the door. Sweetheart,
can we talk about this?" Then my father
saw that I was there.

"Grady, you need to go to your room
for a while."

"What's going on?"

"Your mother is upset."

The chaos behind the door
continued. My father flinched with each
blow.

"Where's Emile?"

"He's in his bedroom."

"What's wrong with Mom?"

"We'll talk later. For now you need
to go to your room." At that my mother
burst out of the bedroom door.

With the door now open, my father,
whose hand had remained against the top
of it while he spoke to me, fell toward my
mother.

"Don't touch me!" she screamed.

Nothing Here is Real

"Marty, where are you going? What are you going to do?"

"I'll tell you what I'm going to do. I'm going over to that psycho's house, and I'm going to ask him just what he thinks he's doing with my son."

"Sweetheart, we ought to let the authorities ask those questions."

"What are you afraid of, Frank? Jesus! Do you think the old man's going to hurt me? What kind of man hears that story from his son and just sits there taking it?"

It was then I realized the reason my parents were shouting at each other; there was a deafening volume of music coming from Emile's room.

"Now," my mother continued, wiping the tears away from her scarlet face, "either you get in that room and talk to your son, or this marriage is over."

"Where are you going?" my father asked.

"Where do you think?" she said as she stormed past us.

My father raised his hands to his chest with his palms opened in a gesture of surrender, but otherwise made no move to stop her. After she was gone, he stood looking silently at the space where she had been. Then, without letting his eyes meet mine, he walked down the hall and opened my brother's door.

I cleared the table and did the dishes-it seemed like the only thing to do. By the time the suds and water filled the left side of our divided sink, the music from my brother's room had faded away.

In a flurry of action my mother opened the door, walked in and rushed toward me. "My God, Grady, I'm so sorry. I'm so sorry."

"It's okay, Mom. What happened?" She was weeping uncontrollably. I felt her weight suddenly shift. She slid down to her knees, her arms wrapped tightly around my legs. I stepped out of her grasp as she continued to sob. "I'll get Dad." But my father was standing in the

doorway. He heard the front door open and
my mother's cries and had left my brother
to attend to his wife.

"What happened, Marty? Did he hurt
you?"

My mother sat on her hip on the
kitchen floor. Her knees were bent and
her feet were kicked out behind her. She
looked like a medieval lady in waiting,
gazing at her own reflection in a pool,
ripe with golden fish. "No, Frank," my
mother looked up from the ground. "He
hurt himself." By the time my father had
picked up the phone to call the police,
Emile had joined us in the kitchen.

The police found Ward Gregory,
just where my mother said they would. My
father brought cups of coffee to the table
as the officers questioned my mother
about what she had seen.

She had knocked first, of course,
but hearing no answer she let herself
in. Drop cloths covered the furniture.
Two sawhorses were set up in the living
room supporting a sheet of pressed

particleboard. An open can of sage green
paint sat next to a soiled brush. The top
of the can was upside down and kicked
sideways on the low-pile, cream carpet
so that a smear of green streaked a path
to the kitchen. The phone was off the
hook and dangled, buzzing incessantly,
from its cord. She called his name, even
announced her intentions as she made
her way up the stairs, but there was no
reply.

She found his bed unmade and
surrounded on the three open sides by
easels, on which sat canvases in various
stages of completion. A variety of brushes
were tossed over the bed sheets. Crinkled
tubes of paint and palates dabbed with
a myriad of color combinations were
scattered all over the bedroom floor.
In the upstairs bathroom she found
the tub full of still-steaming water, a
patterned towel folded on the counter by
the sink next to a straight razor, a can
of Barbasol, and a porcelain mug, which
held a horse-haired lathering brush.

Nothing Here is Real

There was a finger-smear of blood on the mirror.

Nervous now, she passed the second bedroom, glancing in only long enough to see that the shades were drawn, the bed was made, and he wasn't waiting for her there. She made her way down the back stairway that led into the attached garage. This is where she found him.

He had used a string of clothesline to secure his body to the garage door opener. The stepladder was kicked out below his dangling feet. He wore only a pair of urine-stained boxer-briefs. Blood oozed from the fingertips of his right hand where the razor had cut him. His face was too gruesome to describe, she said, but she could tell by the fact that his body still swayed gently to the rhythm of the creaking line against door's pulley system that he hadn't been hanging there long.

She talked without pause, as the men around the table and my brother and I, who gathered out of sight in the hallway, listened in awe. When she seemed to be done, an officer interjected.

"Mrs. Pickett... it's Marty, right?"

She nodded.

"Marty, thank you. We won't trouble you any longer. We just need to know one more thing." My mother looked up slowly at the officer. "Why were you in the house?"

Silence.

"Why did you go there to begin with?" he repeated.

My father answered for her. "My boys mow his lawn for him. The last time Emile, my oldest boy, went there, Gregory hadn't paid him. He was giving my son the runaround--something about weeding the garden before he got paid, so Marty went over to get his back wages for him."

My mother looked at my father, astonished at the dexterity of his dishonesty, and nodded in agreement. "There's no need to question my son," she said. "That's what happened."

"Oh, we won't question your boy unless we have to, Marty. We like to keep

the kids out of stuff like this." We heard
their chairs push back against the floor
of the dining room. "Bill here'll just
finish up the statement, and you can
sign it. Is there anything else you folks
think we need to know?"

"No," my father said.

In the shadows I turned to look
at my brother. He met my gaze, and then
walked silently away. As I followed Emile
down the hall with my eyes, I noticed the
phone cord snaking down the margin of
the hallway and disappearing under his
bedroom door. After he told my parents
everything and my mother exploded with
rage, Emile had obviously called someone.
He didn't have any friends. There was
only one person it could have been.
"I hope you're happy," he said, before
disappearing into the darkness of his
room.

- G. Pickett

Apollo, NY - August 27, 2010

MEETINGS

1.

When Grady saw his Gatsby notes splayed out on the desk, he hesitated a moment before asking the first question of the year.

"'Richard Cory.' Anyone ever hear of it?"

Chances were slim he had to admit. In nine years of teaching he had discovered that, among all of the things he found profoundly important—things students seemed to willfully train themselves to deem irrelevant—poetry was receding in the rearview of kids' consciousness most precipitously.

"Isn't that a song?" The reply came from the brunette girl in the back of the room.

"What's your name?" He realized as he asked that he had been in front of the room for going on five minutes, silently staring at the blank walls and equally blank faces of the students without taking attendance or introducing himself as their teacher.

"I'm Mindy Cole," she said.

"I thought you changed your last name to 'Johnson,' if you know what I mean," snipped a boy with broad shoulders who, despite the fact that class had started, was still sitting on the window sill on the side of the room with his feet on the chair of the desk in front of him.

"Shut up, asshole." The effect of the curse reverberated in the now silent room.

"Look," Grady sighed, fully aware that every eye was watching him, waiting to assess, based exclusively on how he dealt with the girl's cursing tongue, just what kind of teacher they had drawn. "Whatever is going on between you two, knock it off." The girl silently settled into her chair. The boy did not move.

"Sit in a chair like a normal person, will you?" Grady half-heartedly commanded the boy. Then turning to the brunette, before his command could be shrugged off in open defiance, "That's right, Mindy, 'Richard Cory,' the poem written by Edwin Arlington Robinson . . ." As he spoke slowly, Grady held an imaginary pen in his right hand and made a writing motion across his left hand, which he held in front of him like an open book. He was pleased to see that some of the students took the hint and were scurrying to get their own notes out so they could write down what he was saying. "'Richard Cory' was made into a song by Simon and Garfunkel. Anybody know what the song is about?" Another hand shot up in the air. This time it was a boy with dark-rimmed glasses sitting next to Mindy.

"It's about some rich guy who kills himself, right? I'm Reed by the way."

"Thanks, Reed," Grady nodded. "And yes, it is about that in part, but it's about other things as well." He scanned the room to see if anyone would take the bait. Silence.

"Looks like Ms. Johnson and her friend are the only ones who've heard of it. Maybe we could move on to other things. Like, who are you, for instance? My schedule says I'm supposed to have Mrs. Alford for English his year." Grady turned to face the boy by the window again, who despite the previous invitation had yet to take his seat.

Grady slid off his desk, walked over, and after looking into the boy's vacant eyes for a noticeable beat, said, "I must have missed the paperwork on my desk informing me that I have students with learning disabilities in my class this year." A series of muffled giggles broke out behind him. "That's got to be it, right? There's no way you'd be this much of a prick on the first day of school unless you were just too dumb to know otherwise." The boy's cheeks turned scarlet. "Now sit in your seat."

"Hey, you can't talk to me that way."

"And you can't act that way in my classroom, and you know it. So take a seat like I asked you to a minute ago, and we'll call it even." Grady took a step back and waited for the boy to sit down, which he reluctantly did. Grady spun around and walked back to the front of the room. "What were we saying before Mr..." Hoping for an introduction, Grady snapped his fingers and pointed at the boy by the window.

"Seamus. Seamus Clelland," the boy said. "If you're from anywhere near Apollo, you've probably heard of my father."

"Seamus, why don't you just shut up, okay? No one cares who your father is." This time, even though it came from Mindy's side of the room, the comment belonged to the fetching girl sitting in front of her.

"And what's your name?" Grady asked. "Maybe that's where we should start. What do you guys say?" Grady smiled and opened his arms to the rest of the class. "Do you think we can get through attendance without a brawl ensuing?" The nervous laughter that followed told him the rest of the class was anxious to break the tension and get on with things.

"I'm Sophie Standeven," she smiled. "And unless she's hiding something, I'm willing to bet you don't know my mother." It was a well-delivered line, as much a shot at the petulant boy by the window as it was a plea for classroom peace.

"Fair enough," Grady smiled.

"Yeah, but who are you?" Seamus asked again, not totally willing to give up his defiant tone.

"I'm Mr. Pickett. I've been teaching English for the past nine years at Hemlock Hill Academy in Massachusetts. It's a private boarding school. Mrs. Alford decided to stay home with her new daughter, so I'll be in for her this year."

"So you're a sub?" Seamus asked.

Understanding the implications of the question Grady nodded and said, "Yes, mine is a one-year appointment, but either way I'll be your teacher of record, and like I said before, this will be my tenth year teaching."

"What, did you get canned from you private school or something?"

Grady stared at Seamus a beat before deciding to answer the question as if it had been asked without malice. "I'm from Apollo. When I heard about the one-year sub position, it seemed like a good opportunity to give moving back here a chance, while still being able to do what I love, which is teaching English."

"But what about your job in Massachusetts?"

"They've got a kid right out of college teaching my classes this year. Otherwise, they're holding the job for me." Grady looked around the room at the other students who stared blankly back at him. "Now that you all know who I am and where I come from, how about we get back to

English class. Is that all right with you, Mr. Clelland?"

"You're the boss," Seamus laughed, looking to the boys on either side of him, happy he had wasted as much class time as he had.

Falling into rhythm, Grady systematically went around the room asking the students' names and marking them off on his attendance roster. Then he passed out the course syllabus and read it to the students. There were three minutes left in the class when he finished. "Well, it seems we won't be getting to Mr. Robinson's poem today after all, Mr. Clelland." Grady smiled as he addressed Seamus for the first time since their confrontation. "But you did make a good point earlier."

"How's that?" the boy asked, emboldened once again.

"You were correct in pointing out that the majority of your classmates seem to be unfamiliar with the poem I'd like to start the year with. This gives me a great idea. Let's make that a homework assignment." Grady nodded, again mimicking the writing motion of pen and paper with his hands. Go online, find, read, and mark up a copy of Edwin Arlington's poem 'Richard Cory.' Repeat the process with the lyrics to Simon and Garfunkel's song by the same name." There were some groans, but for the most part the students wrote down the assignment. Seamus Clelland, however, just sat at his desk with his arms folded across his chest, shaking his head and glowering at Grady.

The bell rang and the students filed wordlessly out of the room. It wasn't until the door was closed behind the last of them that Grady noticed his hands were shaking.

"Don't you just hate to see that?" The voice caused Grady to jump as he stood in front of the cafeteria. He turned to see Crosby Gibbons, the paint-splattered art teacher, who having arrived twenty minutes late for the first day's lunch duty silently planted himself next Grady in the hope of feigning a constant presence. Crosby was pointing to a snarly-haired boy who sat alone at one of the tables closest to the main hallway. "I had that kid in class second period." Crosby continued, "They stuck me with all freshmen this year—can you believe it?" Though he was new to the building, Grady had already heard rumblings about the controversy brewing in the art department. Knowing what he knew about how things are done at schools, he wasn't surprised to hear that his colleague was suffering through this form of indirect punishment.

Crosby Gibbons had taught art at Eden Heights for the past twenty-five years. With seniority and professional accomplishments to his credit, he'd been assigned the Advanced Placement course for the past ten years. The AP course was the envy of every art teacher in the building, mostly because it was usually occupied by students who, with little instruction and minimal prodding, could be left to their own devices and still produce halfway decent art. This, of course, allowed an artist like Gibby, as he was known throughout the district, to spend the day, not instructing, but rather plying his own trade on the school's dime. In fact Gibby was foolish enough to brag, after downing a few drinks at last year's Christmas party, that some of his best work had been produced in his "Eden Heights studio," while his students were working on "whatever shit they were trying to produce."

His comments rubbed Steve Donovan, the art department chair, the wrong way. Donovan and Gibby had had their differences over the years, and it was no secret that Donovan wanted nothing more than to get Gibby out of the AP classes—classes Donovan was sure he was better suited to teach. Gibby was largely untouchable at Eden Heights, one because of the quality of art his students produced and two because he was one of the most recognized artists in Buffalo's trendy downtown art scene. But when Donovan overheard Gibby's drunken boast and relayed it back to Artie Morris, the high school principal, there was no way for Gibby to avoid the heat.

It had been Donovan's wish that his and Gibby's

schedule be switched for the second semester, but Artie Morris refused. The principal did, however, admit Gibby was out of line in bragging about taking advantage of the school, and given the public nature of his comments, they couldn't go without action. Gibby, still high off the morning joint he had shared with a student in the old darkroom attached to the back of his classroom, had lip-farted at Artie's attempt at asserting his authority and simply said, "Do whatever you've got to do, man." Artie Morris obliged.

"Ten years I've been teaching the AP kids, and this year, out of the blue, that fruitcake Morris gives me all freshmen."

"Sucks."

"Yeah, but not as much as this duty," the old man said.

"Ah, I don't know," Grady shrugged. "It's not so bad when you're only here for half of it."

"Was I late?" Gibby grinned back. Then suddenly serious he said, "Listen, I'm sure we met during the opening meetings and all, but I've forgotten your name. Where're you from?"

Grady looked in the direction of the clock before answering. "I didn't come to any of the opening meetings. I just got back into town. I've been teaching out in Massachusetts. I'm in for Betsy Alford this year. A one-year sub position." He extended his hand, "Grady Pickett. I'm from Apollo originally."

Crosby shook his hand and paused waiting for Grady to say more. When he didn't, Gibby said, "Big happenings this fall in Apollo."

"Oh yeah, what's that?"

"You're telling me you haven't heard about the Ward Gregory show opening in town?"

"Oh, right. That." Grady shrugged.

"Well, it's not every day paintings by an artist of his caliber just show up however many years after the guy dies. And how can you not like the guy? His early stuff is amazing."

"You know what's funny?" Grady said. "Just yesterday I saw a For Rent sign in his old apartment on Water Street. If you like him so much, you should check it out."

"Shit, I wouldn't step foot in that place if you paid me."

"Why's that?"

"C'mon. It's no secret it's haunted."

"I never noticed any ghosts," Grady laughed.

"You've been in that apartment?"

"No, but I've been by it enough. Besides, that wasn't where he lived when he died."

"I know that," Gibby said shortly. "But if you knew the whole story, you wouldn't be joking about it. Let's just leave it at that."

"Fair enough." Grady chuckled, happy to be distracted by the banter. "Hey," he said, "speaking of mysteries, see that kid over there?" Grady pointed a finger in the direction of Seamus Clelland, who was sitting at what clearly was the table of choice.

"Clelland," Gibby barked. "His father's bad news. The kid's not much better from what I've seen. Never had him in class, but I know the dad pretty well. He's an Apollo guy too. You should know him."

"That's what the kid said in class today."

"How'd that come up?" Gibby asked as the bell rang.

"I've got to get to class," Grady replied. "I'll tell you tomorrow."

"That's if I haven't quit this shit by then," Gibby shouted over his shoulder.

2.

When he pulled into his parents' driveway, Grady saw that his father was home.

"How'd the apartment search go?" Frank asked as Grady climbed the three steps into the kitchen, surprised to see his father holding the door.

"I didn't have any time to look today, Dad."

"Long day, huh?"

"No. Not so bad, I guess." His father had started the water boiling and was sizzling some seasoned meat for the sauce.

"Spaghetti all right? Mom left a note. She won't be home until 9:00, so I figure we'd do the bachelor feast."

"Yeah, spaghetti's fine. Thanks." A modest stack of unopened mail sat on the kitchen table. "What's this?" Grady asked, picking up the copy of The Apollo Sun, which was folded twice and placed strategically on top of the pile.

"There's an article there about the woods you and Emile used to play in. I figured you'd want to see it. They're talking of tearing them down."

"Tearing down Worthingdale Woods?"

"Yep. I guess *nothing gold can stay . . .*"

Grady smiled. His father was not a poet, but when Grady declared his intent to major in English, Frank asked him for some reading suggestions. That Christmas, Grady gave him a tattered, used copy of The Complete Works of Robert Frost. Ever since then Frank had been quoting lines of Frost's poetry to his son, just to let him know that he had actually read it.

"Why would they tear them down?"

"Development. Houses. Prefab homes, a cul-de-sac. They've got a picture of the drawings posted on the board in the foyer of the school. That's what the article says anyway. I haven't been in that school for years."

"Another house farm?"

"I know. I figured you'd be upset, but I thought you'd want to know. They haven't decided they'll do it for sure. There's a meeting about it tonight. I thought maybe you'd want to go. I imagine Emile might be there. Might be a good chance for you two to reconnect. You guys haven't touched base since you got back into town, right?"

"Look, I'll be down for dinner, okay?" Grady went upstairs to change his clothes, the rolled up newspaper shoved in the back pocket of his khakis.

With the door of his room closed he unrolled the paper and read the article in its entirety. His father was right. The plan to cut down the woods was in its final stages of approval. Two house-lined cul-de-sacs were to be put in its place. The project would take two years to complete. The schedule was set, the building contract had been granted to Veteran Renewal—described in the article as "a development company with local ties." All that remained to be done before the trees began to fall was for the town board to vote on the proposal. There was a scheduled public hearing tonight. The vote would be next week.

By the time Grady finished reading the article and changing his clothes, he was certain he couldn't stomach dinner. His father frowned, but thankfully didn't ask any questions when Grady asked him to save his spaghetti. Then, grabbing his windbreaker, Grady headed out of the house and down the block toward Worthingdale Woods.

The Apollo town board met twice a month, usually in the upper meeting room of the town hall, but due to the expected crowd, that night's meeting was moved to the public library. The library closed early for the occasion, and extra chairs were brought down from the high school to meet the seating need. For several months the board had tried to contain the news that the woods might come down, only discussing the possibility at the sparsely attended planning sessions the first Tuesday of each month, and then pushing the development discussion off the agenda of the public meetings held the third Tuesday of the month. But the board knew if a vote were announced without a chance to publicly quell the naysayers, the whole thing could fall through. The article in the paper was the compromise. If you appear transparent, people will think you have nothing to hide. The meeting was scheduled for 8:30 p.m. By 8:00 p.m. there was a line formed half way around the block. Apollo did not take kindly to change.

Grady was one of the first people in line, mostly because he wanted to avoid returning to his parents' house and trying to explain to his father why he had spent the last two hours walking aimlessly around the town.

As Grady scanned the room for familiar faces, he was stunned to see his student Seamus Clelland enter through the door and take a seat in the back of the room. Grady was all set to ask the woman next to him, who looked as though he should know her, to save his seat so he could go ask his student what he was doing in Apollo when the meeting was called to order and the board members sauntered in. When the last of the board members entered the room Grady knew why his student was there.

Even at a distance of twelve feet, Grady could clearly see in the face of Keith Clelland, the last board member to enter the room, the same furtive darkness he saw in Seamus's eyes earlier that day. The meeting began, but Grady was oblivious to the goings on. Instead, he stared at the man who sat in the front of the room, trying his best to place him in his memory until a crisp, familiar voice broke through.

"I appreciate that Mr. Clelland, in addition to serving on the board, is a decorated war veteran and owner of a local business, not to mention a long time resident of Apollo, but if you heard, outside of the context of Apollo, the circumstances surrounding his company getting the contract would any of you not laugh at the obvious nepotism going on here? He's a member of the board, for God's sake—how can you grant his company the contract?"

It had been years since Grady had seen his high school classmate. They grew up together through the ranks of Apollo's school system. She was the senior class president; he was her vice. During the first year away at college, they had tried to maintain their friendship. One night, while home from break after freshman year, they were at a party together. Grady, high off a few too many beers, tried out some tired lines on his old friend. She floated away from him, but before she left that night, she made a point of coming back over and looking him square in the eyes. "You know, Grady," she said, "I always thought you were a good guy." In his drunken stupor, Grady took that as an invitation, but Susan was gone before the sting from her slap faded. He'd heard she had gone on to law school after college, but he'd lost track of her after that.

"First of all, Ms. Luster," Mark Hartley replied, "please refrain from swearing in this public setting."

"Did I swear?"

"Last I checked, refraining from using the Lord's name in vain is one of the Ten Commandments."

Susan Luster rolled her eyes.

"But more importantly, the proposal is just that, a proposal. All aspects of it are up for discussion—including the use of Mr. Clelland's company. That's why we're here. Now please, let us try to remain rational in our comments. Is there anyone else who would like to add anything to this meeting?" Exasperated, Susan sat down, picked up a legal pad off the floor and began scribbling madly.

Clelland was talking now. "First of all, I'd like to point out here that, and correct me if I'm mistaken, Sue, Ms. Luster, is no longer a resident of Apollo. You live with your mother in the Nottingham apartments in Eden Heights now. Isn't that right?"

Susan's faced reddened, and she stood to defend herself. Clelland benevolently raised his hand. "Now I know you moved in with her to care for her—even gave up your place in town here. That's sweet, but the fact remains this is a public hearing for residents of Apollo. I'll kindly ask you to remember that." A murmur went through the crowd. Susan spoke above Mark Hartley's reprimand that she stay seated.

"I'll have you know, Keith, that my place here in town is still on the market, so like it or not, I'm technically a resident. And you can keep your comments about my personal life to yourself."

Keith pushed himself back from the table and raised his hands in mock-surrender, then smiled toward Mark Hartley and mouthed the words, "I tried."

"Again folks, let's try to keep this civil," Hartley said after rapping the gavel on the table for order. "Are there any comments about the project itself?"

Grady was listening half-heartedly as Susan and Clelland exchanged their verbal blows. He was more interested in doing math. Keith Clelland was familiar, but from where? There was no way they were in school together. Grady was sure of that. How could he be a veteran? What war was Susan talking about? We'd gone to war with Iraq in 2002. Could he have been in the army then? What's more, Seamus Clelland was at least sixteen. Had to be. That meant if Keith Clelland was his father, he became his father when he was just a kid himself. It just didn't add up, but it had to. It had to.

The gavel pounded again as a red-faced woman on the other side of the room sat down. Grady recognized her kind face as that of Ellen Hardy, the long time Worthingdale Elementary School secretary.

"Mrs. Hardy," Keith smiled, "I'm a hunter. I love the outdoors just as much as anybody, and I can appreciate the sentiment behind your comments. I can also understand that you must have spent hours upon hours over the years watching the seasons change from your desk there in the office. But, Mrs. Hardy, I promise you, we'll build pretty houses. The cutest houses you've ever seen. We'll even plant trees. Save some of the ones already there. You don't have to worry about taste with us. We've got it. The thing we ought to be talking about is jobs and local income. These are the things at stake here. If this project doesn't go through, think of the hit the tax base will take."

"That's fuzzy math." Susan Luster spoke from the crowd.

Mark Hartley stood and pointed the gavel at her. "Ms. Luster you speak out of turn again, and you'll be asked to leave. Now, anyone have anything to say about Keith's last point?"

"I do." Grady was standing with his hand in air. Hartley sat down and nodded in Grady's direction.

"I'm Grady Pickett. I grew up here. I've been away

Nothing Here is Real

for a while, but now I'm back. Listen, I can appreciate what Mr. Clelland here is saying about housing and expanding the tax base and all, and I think he's right to consider what could be lost if this project doesn't go through. But I'd ask that the board also consider what will be lost if those woods are cut down. Let's think about it for a second. One of the reasons Apollo remains a great place to live is that we as a community have resisted the urge to pave everything in sight. Mrs. Hardy is right. That square mile of woods is a source of natural beauty, and we ought to preserve that. It's also teeming with wild life. Deer, fox, birds, even coyotes from time to time. If we cut down those woods, even if we save a few token trees for aesthetics, where will those creatures go? Certainly we value life enough to consider that. And the last thing I'll ask is this: who in this room who's spent anytime at Worthingdale Elementary can't remember playing in those woods? The fact is, those woods are a part of this town's past. To cut them down would saw off a part of ourselves. I beg you not to do it. And certainly not in the name of erecting another soulless house farm. That's the last thing this world needs."

Grady sat as applause erupted around him. Hartley slammed his gavel down on the table. "Enough, enough. This isn't a rally. It's a meeting." Keith Clelland was trying his best to get Hartley's attention for a response, but the old man was on a roll. "I think, Mr. Pickett, that we'd all be better off if we refrained from incendiary language. The intention is not to build a 'soulless house farm' as you call it, but a collection of tastefully constructed homes. If you had taken the time to review the publicly posted plans, you would have seen that."

"Yes, another hand. Forgive me, I can't see quite that far. Who owns the hand in the back?" Mark Hartley asked.

"Emile Pickett. I assume, unlike my prodigal brother, I don't need an introduction." Grady turned in his seat. He hadn't laid eyes on Emile in over a year.

"Okay then, Emile. What do you have to say?" Hartley asked.

"It's pretty clear my brother spent too much time when he was away in Massachusetts reading Henry David Thoreau." Grady felt the back of his neck redden. "Those woods aren't any sort of sanctuary or whatever he said. They're a public menace. How many of the same people who claim those woods as some wonderland of childhood can also say they had their first cigarette there, or took their first drink there, or maybe even did something worse there? Any takers? I know you won't raise your hand to those questions, but we all know it's true." Emile paused long enough to look directly at Grady, and then raising his hand in his brother's direction he continued.

"Now maybe, in the time that he's been away, my brother has come to see things like hunting and new construction as contrary to the Apollo way. But as a patriot and lifelong resident of this town, I support Keith Clelland and his proposal. Keep it local. Let the village grow."

There was a spattering of applause at Emile's comments. Making a gun with his thumb and forefinger, Keith Clelland pointed it in the direction of Grady's brother, winked his eye and clicked his mouth in chorus before Emile sat down.

"Okay, now that we've heard from the Picketts, shall we continue?"

Grady turned around in his seat and sought out his brother's eyes. How had he missed Emile in the line coming in? When he found his brother in the crowd, he saw that he was sitting next to his wife Sarah, looking directly at Grady. Grady raised his hands and eyebrows at once. His brother smiled, nodded and mouthed the words, "You lose." Grady shook his head and turned around as Hartley banged the gavel against the table a final time. Without further comment, the meeting was adjourned.

Grady caught his brother's shoulder as Emile leaned into his car. Emile stood quickly and yanked his arm away. "Can I help you?"

"What the hell was all that?"

"I was stating my position. Welcome back."

"Whatever your problem is, that's fine. I just would appreciate your keeping in mind that I've got to live in this town, too, at least for the next year."

"Oh, I see. It's fine for you to slander me? And I'm just supposed to sit there and take it, right? Because little broken-hearted brother has just come back to town?"

"What the hell are you talking about? I didn't slander you."

"No? What were you talking about then Grady? What was all that poetic shit about childhood and animals?"

"Emile, I wasn't talking about your past. I was just saying..."

"Spare me. I've been surprised by your betrayals before, but never again. Besides, you're the last person in the world who should be saying anything about stopping a beating heart."

"What the hell does that mean?"

"I know how you work, Grady. What'll it be first, the deer? The accident?"

"Emile, I . . ."

His brother cut him off. "See, I know you better

than you know yourself. But I'm not afraid of the past. You can't use it against me. I've been forgiven. And besides, I know the truth about why you came running home from Massachusetts. I've made some calls."

"Some calls? What's that supposed to mean?"

"Yes. When Mom told me you were moving back but wouldn't tell her why, I made some calls."

"Really? Who'd you call?"

Ignoring his question Emile continued. "The point is I know the truth. And to my way of thinking, it's about time some other people knew it as well."

"Is that some kind of threat?"

Emile laughed. "The fact is the Vita Coalition and I have got a job to do in this town, and nothing is going to stop us from doing it."

"I don't know what the hell you're talking about half the time."

"That's right you don't," Emile said, and with that he ducked into the car, threw it into gear, and roared out of the parking lot, sending pedestrians scattering on the way.

Grady walked to his car alone, looking after Emile in amazement. "Brothers, huh?" he heard from behind him.

Turning, his eyes met those of his classmate, Susan

Luster. "Hey, Susan."

"Pure Apollo. It's almost like the old battles we used to have with the high school administration about getting a vending machine for the cafeteria."

"It's crazy what was important back then, isn't it?"

"How you doing?" she said.

"Pretty good. Take it all around. Kind of a crazy day today, but yeah, I'm okay on the whole." He looked at her now, determined to shake off his encounter with Emile. "You look great. How've you been?"

She wrapped her arms around him in a chaste embrace. Then, ignoring his question she said, "It's been forever. I mean, I haven't seen you in, like, years. What brings you back? Certainly you didn't just come swooping out of nowhere to defend the Worthingdale Woods."

"Uh, no," Grady laughed. "Nothing like that. I moved back is all. I've taken a one-year sub position at Eden Heights. The plan is I'll go back to Hemlock Hill, where I've been teaching in Massachusetts, at the end of the year, but for now, let's just say, it was the right time for me to get some distance from the place." Susan looked at him silently, waiting for Grady to fill in the blanks. "Anyway," he continued, "I'm living with my parents until I find another place."

"They're still in town?"

"Yeah. Same as always."

"And so is Emile."

"Emile will never leave."

"It's funny," she said, "every once in a while I'll see his name in the paper. Letters to the editor mostly."

"He's got a lot of opinions. Always has."

"Yeah, what was that all about in there? 'My prodigal brother.'"

"Oh, Nothing. Like you said, just brothers, I guess." Grady looked at the ground searching for something to say. "Hey, by the way, any idea what the Vita Coalition is?"

"They're that crazy pro-life group. Your brother basically runs it. You're telling me you didn't know about that?"

"No. I've sort of been out of the loop, you know."

"I guess."

Grady coughed into his hand. "But anyway, I'm serious, what have you been doing?" he asked again.

"Oh, you mean aside from getting scolded at meetings?" she laughed. "Nothing. I'm a lawyer." Then, without saying more she looked at her watch and said, "Hey, what do you say we finish this conversation over a drink at The Well? I could use a beer."

Grady opened the sedan's door. "I didn't think you drank."

"Come on," Susan said, holding the door open as Grady climbed into the seat. "Seriously, let's go grab a beer."

"I've got to work tomorrow. I'll be teaching Gatsby to angry juniors at 7:30 in the morning."

"Gatsby, huh? 'Can't repeat the past? Why of course you can.' Wasn't that it?"

"Nice memory."

"No, my book club went through a classics phase last year." She smirked as he closed the door. She turned away for a moment as he pulled the seat belt across his chest. There was a knock on the window. Grady lowered it, and Susan handed him a crumpled slip of paper. "I feel like a kid doing this, but that's the number at my mom's. I'm staying there most of the time now. You should give me a call sometime."

"You know, Susan," Grady grinned, "I always thought you were a good girl."

3.

They were two weeks into their reading of The Great Gatsby when Grady walked in one morning and handed each of his students a copy of a sloppily written essay. The topic was Tim O'Brien's short story "On the Rainy River."

"What's this?" Seamus asked after the bell rang. "Did I miss something yesterday?"

"No." Grady smiled at the fact that no matter the circumstance, Seamus Clelland found a way to strike an offensive position. "No, this is an essay a student I had in my first year of teaching wrote in the last month of his senior year. I want you to read it and tell me what you think. Don't worry. You don't need to have read the story it's about to get it." The students dutifully ducked their heads and began reading.

After ten minutes Logan's hand went up in the air. Despite the fact Grady could tell not everyone was finished reading, Grady called on him. "What grade did you say this guy was in?"

"He was a senior when he wrote this essay."

"I'm not a great writer," Ty started, "but this essay is

horrible. Every other word is misspelled."

"More than that," Chaz added. "It doesn't make any sense. I mean, I'm a pretty smart guy, and I can't follow it all."

"Yeah, I may not be as smart as Chaz," Seamus mocked, "But all of the sentences seem out of order. What's the deal? Was this kid like a retard or something?" The last of his comments caused his cronies to chuckle.

"Seamus, your inappropriate comment aside, you ask a good question. It's important to know the context here. I should probably tell you about the boy who wrote this essay. But before I do that, I want you to tell me what you know about him." Grady flipped on the projector, and a huge picture of an athletic boy with a charming smile and strikingly congruent facial features jumped up on the screen. "This is Justin Backhaus, the author of the essay you hold in your hands. What can you tell me about him?"

"Player," Sophie blurted out.

"Yeah," Michelle Seibolt agreed. "He looks like one of those guys who's gotten by on his looks. You know, charms all of his female teachers, makes buddies with all the guys. A hundred bucks says he's a jock."

"What makes you so sure, Michelle?" Grady asked.

"Seamus is right," she said. "This essay is horrible."

"So what does that have to do with anything you

said?"

"Well," Sophie interrupted, "he just looks so happy. Like he doesn't have a care in the world. I know if I were dumb enough to write an essay this bad when I was senior, I wouldn't be smiling."

"Maybe he doesn't know any better?" Chaz said reasonably. "Maybe he's one of those kids who doesn't care about school but has a great deal of charisma that he'll get by on all of his life." He was looking at Seamus as he made his last comment.

"I probably should tell you a few things about Justin, before we get too far into this," Grady said. "Justin went to the boarding school I taught at in Massachusetts. He was the captain of the football team."

"I knew it," Michelle blurted out.

Grady continued, "He was, at the time this essay was written, planning on going to Cornell the next year." Grady paused and then asked, "What do you think?"

"Planning on going, or accepted?" Chaz asked with a sense of desperation in his voice.

"He was going to Cornell."

"That changes things. I mean, obviously he blew this assignment off. How else can you explain it, right?" asked Ty.

"Either that or he was going to Cornell to play

football," Sophie reasoned.

"Cornell is an Ivy League school. My father went to Cornell," Chaz stammered. "They don't just let meatheads in there."

Seamus smiled. "I bet he got in because of his dad. You know how those old boys' clubs work. It was an insider's job for sure."

"I resent that," Chaz shouted.

"Relax dude," Logan said. "He's just kidding."

"Let's get back to Justin, shall we?" Grady said pulling the class back in. "Here's something else you should know. Justin Backhaus was the valedictorian of his class."

"That solves it."

"What do you mean, Sophie?"

"I mean, no offense, but he obviously didn't take your class seriously. That or he didn't read and was just BS'ing on the test."

"People do that?" Grady asked in mock horror. "On essay tests?" The class laughed at his sarcasm. "Okay, so maybe that's it. The star athlete, who also happens to be a scholar, blows off an assignment. No big deal, right? We all have failed to take something seriously from time to time, right?" Heads nodded around the room. "So how do you feel now about the judgment you passed on him just a few minutes ago, knowing what you know now about

Justin?"

"Well, you set us up," said Michelle.

"Yeah, you made it so we'd judge him. That wasn't fair." Sophie seemed genuinely hurt.

"Wait a minute, Ms. Standeven. All I did was give you this essay and show you his picture. You judged him all on your own."

"So what's the point?" Logan asked losing his patience.

"What if I took one of your essays, saved it, and handed it out to students ten years later, then showed them your picture and asked them what they thought? Would you be happy with what they said?"

"You can't just do that, can you?" Michelle seemed concerned. "Like, isn't that an invasion of privacy? It seems like you're selling the kid out or something."

"I can see why you'd say that, and I'd probably agree, but I asked Justin's mother if I could use the essay in class, and she gave me permission."

"Why didn't you ask him?" Logan asked. "I know my mother would love it if I got embarrassed every year for the rest of my life, if I blew an assignment off, but I sure as hell would say no if you asked me for permission."

Grady was silent for a moment, and then he said, "Justin was killed by a drunk driver the day after he wrote this essay. He didn't graduate. He didn't go to Cornell to play football and pursue his engineering degree. He died on the side of the road. He was out for a run. His girlfriend of two years, Becky McCormick, had dumped him earlier in the day, so when he got back to the dorm he decided he would skip lacrosse practice and go for a run to blow off some steam.

"The guy that hit him was so hammered he just kept on driving. In court he swore that he thought he hit a deer. The only reason Justin's body was found so quickly was because his coach reported him as missing from practice. Eventually, they got it out of his roommate that he had gone out for a run. The dean found the skid marks on the road and called the cops. Justin was still alive when they found him, but not for long." Grady looked around the room. All of the students were looking down at their desks. Even Seamus.

"Are we what we do? Do our actions define us?" Grady let the questions linger. "Justin wrote this essay just a few hours before he died. His entire academic career was defined by excellence, but this essay, which he wrote having just been dumped by his girlfriend, was his parting shot. His last essay. Can we judge him based upon it?"

"No," Sophie asserted. "Absolutely not."

"But he wrote it, Sophie. It's there on paper."

"But come on, Mr. Pickett. There's more to the story. There's more than what's there."

"But that is what he did. This essay is his lasting monument. We are what we do."

"Justin Backhaus isn't this essay anymore than I'm this outfit or you're this lesson." Mindy Cole's first words of the day were delivered with a flat, even tone.

"Okay, Ms. Cole. If we aren't what we do, what are we? What we think? What we want to do? What defines us as people?"

All of the eyes in the room were on Mindy. "All I know is it's impossible to take any given moment out of context and judge it. When you do that, you get what happened during the first few minutes of class today. You've got to look at the whole picture. We are what we do, but also what we think, what we feel, all of it. You've got to consider everything."

"Is that really realistic?"

"We have to see it all," she shrugged. "It's that simple."

Then, holding up his copy of The Great Gatsby, Grady asked, "What about Daisy? How do we judge her?"

The class was silent again. "Do we judge her on what she does, what she thinks, whom she's with, whom she leaves behind? How about Gatsby? Do his actions

define him? He gives up everything for Daisy. His life is
defined by trying to win her back, right? So that must mean
he loves her. His actions say he does. Or do they?" The
students were shuffling restlessly in their desks. Seeing that
none of them were willing to bite at his questions, he said,
"Take out your books. I'd like you to read Chapter Seven
for homework tonight. It's a big one, so read it with today's
discussion in mind. You can go ahead and get started." He
made his way to his desk, sat down and opened his own
copy to the beginning of the assigned chapter, unsure of
why his heart was racing.

The balled-up sandwich flew across the room
and skidded to a stop in front of the boy sitting alone at
the table by the hallway. It was twenty minutes into the
period, and Gibby had yet to show up. Under normal
circumstances, Grady would have deployed his colleague,
who so far seemed more than willing to follow Grady's lead
on all matters related to their shared duty, to discover who
threw the sandwich while Grady tried to attend to the boy
on the receiving end of the used lunch meat, but Gibby
wasn't there.

Colin Mitchell was the boy's name. It had taken
two weeks for Grady to get that out of him. Grady noticed
him alone on the first day of school, and Crosby Gibbons

confirmed that the skinny boy was a loner, but both men underestimated the degree to which both Colin's physical stature and his seat of choice in the cafeteria would motivate the table of cool-guy freshmen to harass him.

Every day for the past two weeks Grady had spent his lunch period alternating between trying to catch the table of taunting boys in the act of whatever indignity they were dreaming up and reaching out to the poor kid who insisted on making an easy target of himself by sitting alone. Grady had tried all means of discipline on the offending table. Each one of the bullies had been given detention and made to stay after to clean up the cafeteria. Grady even called one of their mothers in an act of desperation, but the hazing persisted. It was as if all of his efforts were taken as signs of encouragement. The balled up sandwich Grady now held in his hand marked the latest step in the escalation. The way Grady saw it, if he didn't do something drastic, it was only a matter of time before a full tray of food was thrown at the boy's head.

"Listen," Grady said to the zit-faced, shaggy blonde-haired kid he now stood over, "I saw you throw the sandwich."

"The sandwich... I'm not sure what you mean," the boy countered. The rest of the table erupted in laughter.

"I'm sick of your crap." Grady slammed the

mangled meat down in front of the smiling boy. "Come with me." Grady grabbed him and yanked him out of his seat with such abrupt force that his tray spilled onto the floor.

"Hey, you can't grab me like that! I'll sue," the boy shouted as all of the eyes in the room turned to witness the spectacle.

Grady dragged the boy toward the tables by the window, where Mindy Cole was sitting with some other junior girls. With his free hand, Grady grabbed an empty chair from a passing table, slid it into a vacant spot, and deposited first the chair and then the boy in front of the table of girls. Then taking a breath and looking at the stunned faces of the girls, Grady smiled. "Hello, ladies." The girls nodded. "As you can see this young man is having a hard time adjusting to the high school lunch scene." The girls nodded again. "See, he thinks it's still cool to throw food at lonely kids who are sitting by themselves in front of the room. He thinks that's the best way to get noticed. He doesn't know yet that it's cooler just to chill with your friends during lunch than it is to make some poor kid's life a living hell by heckling him every day. I figured you all could explain to him that it isn't cool to be a bully. I guess I thought if he heard it from a table of pretty girls maybe it would sink in."

"Sure," Mindy answered. "We can do that for you, Mr. Pickett."

"Good." Then, without waiting for further acknowledgment, Grady turned and walked toward the hallway leaving the room full of students to fend for themselves.

4.

Ward Gregory's old apartment needed work. It was at least two years since anyone had lived there on a full-time basis. As Grady followed the elfin agent around the place, he noticed there were brown stains on the drop ceiling, the appliances were filthy and outdated, and the water in the toilet gently swirled even after Grady jiggled the flusher. The forced-air heat blew with such gust out of the register that dust bunnies spun wildly across the gummed up kitchen floor. Just as the realtor noted its habit of shutting off at inopportune times, Grady noticed the second bedroom was covered in what appeared to be bird shit.

"Is that what it looks like?" Grady asked.

"Oh, yes, if by 'that' you mean bird droppings." The agent nodded. "Yes, that's what it is."

Grady walked over to the caked window sill and, using the heel of his hand, pushed open the window to let in the cool early evening air. Then, putting his hand up to see if there was a screen (there wasn't), he leaned his head out the window, doing his best to prevent his clothes from touching the petrified crap.

Nothing Here is Real

"So what's up with the bird shit?" Grady asked.

"Look, you've seen the place, so let me level with you, okay? You seem like a nice guy. I don't want to waste any more of your time." He paused slightly. "This is an intriguing property, but it's obviously a little quirky." Grady stared at the man, waiting for him to fill in the blanks. "This apartment is noteworthy because of the historic significance of its previous occupant." Grady nodded. "But frankly," the agent continued, "it wasn't until the historic nature of the apartment's previous occupant came to light several years ago that the landlord began to have trouble renting the place."

"I'm not sure I get it," Grady said.

"There are some people in this town who believe this apartment has been visited by... shall we say *familiar* spirits.'"

"People think it's haunted, right? I got that."

The agent, now seeing that Grady was familiar with the place, continued more directly. "A few years ago there were some *happenings* here, and then the residents at the time ran into a bit of bad luck. From that they concluded the apartment was haunted. They left without a word to the landlord, but did manage to tell everyone they knew of the apartment's apparent curse. Since that time, the landlord has had a hard time renting it for any sort of extended period of time."

"Okay," sighed Grady, doing his best to play along. "But that doesn't explain why the bedroom is covered in bird shit."

"Oh, well that . . ." the agent continued. "That happened while the last tenant was here. He opened the window one summer night, to let some air in the place, and I guess he forgot there wasn't a screen. Anyway, he went out to The Well for some drinks, and when he came back with his girlfriend, he found that the door to the bedroom was closed, and there were all sorts of noises coming from inside." Then with a flop of his hand the realtor trailed off, hoping Grady would guess the end of the story and save him from telling it again.

"Then what happened?"

"The story goes," the agent said slowly and with an obvious degree of anguish, "that when the girl opened the door she found the room was full of... blackbirds."

"Creepy."

"Yes, well, that's what the couple thought as well. The man moved his stuff out that night and the place has been for rent ever since."

"And all that time the landlord hasn't thought to clean up the mess?"

"It's complicated," the agent explained. "Let's just

say that the landlord's holding out hope for the property to be *re-zoned*. He's got it in his head that after the gallery opens uptown there will be sufficient buzz about the apartment's former occupant that there might be a groundswell of interest in turning the place into some sort of museum. But until that time, he's keeping the For Rent sign in the window. Money is money, you know."

"I get it," Grady said. "Why bother going to the trouble of cleaning the place if you're hoping it won't get rented anyway?"

"Right."

"But it would be cleaned, right? If someone were interested in it?"

"Wait," the agent said. "You're not seriously thinking of taking this place, are you?"

Grady shrugged. "I don't see why not…if you guys'll clean it up."

"Of course, of course. We would give the property a thorough cleaning, which would meet your inspection, before we would expect any sort of security deposit." The agent paused. "I take it you don't believe in ghosts?"

"The guy probably left a half-eaten pizza in the room and forgot there wasn't a screen. Once one crow sees that kind of meal, he gets the word out to his buddies, and it's party-time." Then Grady cuffed the agent on the shoulder. "Besides," he said. "I'm used to living with ghosts."

An hour after he left his parents' house for good, Grady called and made plans to meet Susan at The Well. When he got there he found her sitting alone with a pitcher of beer and two empty glasses on the table in front of her. She was wearing a skirt and had pulled her hair back in a way that made her look like she was seventeen again.

She saw him and glancing quickly toward the bar, waved him over to her table. He slid into the open chair, and she said, "You know, I took a big risk ordering this pitcher. If you stood me up, I would have had to take care of it all myself."

"No doubt you could have handled that." Grady smiled back at her, allowing his eyes to take her in fully for the first time in years—her graceful neck, her long, slender fingers, the beauty mark just above the collar of the low-cut top. Yes, she was a beautiful woman. For a moment, Grady felt a stirring in his heart. Would it be so bad to seek some comfort? To bring her home to his bed and hold her in his arms?

"Oh, I don't know. I might have called on my buddy at the bar to help me." As she said this, her eyebrow arched toward the bar. Sitting on the stool closest to the kitchen, surrounded by a handful of empty glasses, was Keith Clelland. He swiveled to order another drink.

"Do you want to go somewhere else?" Grady asked.

"Nah. He's harmless here."

"Seems like there's more to the story with you and Clelland."

"What do you mean?" she asked.

"I mean, at the meeting and all. Did you know I'm teaching his kid? I can't wait for the parent conference. Why the hell does he look so familiar anyway?"

"He was in eighth grade when we were seniors. The only reason I know that, by the way, is that he knocked up my little sister's best friend when they were freshmen. He dropped out of school to work for his old man's construction company for a while after that, but his dad nearly killed him one night, so he moved back in with his mom and ended up graduating a few years later."

"How did he end up on the board?"

"Well, he was only elected last fall. It's kind of a long story."

"Go ahead," Grady said.

"I don't know if you'd remember, but Keith's father Glen used to own a nursery in Eden Heights. It'd been in the family for years."

"Glen Acres?"

"Right, that's what they called it. All the firstborns in the family were named Glen, until Keith came along. Anyway, the Glen that was Keith's father ended up being a class-A screw-up. He split from his wife when Keith was still a kid and ended up hitting the bottle pretty hard." Grady nodded.

"Well, one thing leads to another," Susan continued, "and he ends up losing the business because he runs into trouble with the Environmental Protection Agency for dumping illegal fertilizers into Shenengo Creek."

"What a scumbag."

"Get this," she said grabbing Grady's arm. "He probably would have sat in jail for contempt of court– he wouldn't give the name of the company who sold the chemicals to him—but he served with the judge in Vietnam. He got off on a technicality."

"Unbelievable."

"Right. But he did have to sell the nursery."

"And what does this have to do with Keith being on the board?"

Susan laughed. "Like I said, it's a long story. The business was in his family for years. They'd mulched half of the Southtowns, for God's sake, and Glen Clelland wasn't above giving discounts to people he liked. The point is, they had some very loyal clients, clients who, when they heard Glen was forced to sell the business, made damn sure he wasn't out of work more than six months."

"What do you mean?" Grady asked.

"One of his old clients got him into the construction business—building houses. Clelland made so much on the sale of Glen Acres that he was able to throw his money at developers during the housing boom in Eden Heights. Veteran Renewal built almost every one of those fancy new houses that went up over there during the 80s and 90s. After a while, Glen figures why just get paid to build the houses and instead starts getting into the development side of things."

"What about Keith?"

"The start of the development business was right around the time Keith gets deployed."

"I was trying to figure this out the other night. How did he fight in the war?"

"Yes, he served during the initial surge in Iraq. He was a big time hero in the taking of Bagdad."

"I guess all that rage has to go somewhere, right?"

"Right, only he got blown up by a roadside bomb at the end of it and came home without a left leg. The one he's standing on up there is titanium, they say."

"Titanium?"

"Yeah," Susan nodded. "He won a lot of medals, but it doesn't make him any less of an asshole."

"Anyway, then he comes home, takes up with Marcy again, and starts working with his father on the idea that someday he'll take over the business."

"He's still doing that, right? That's what you said the other night."

"Well, not with his father. See, a year or so after he got back, Glen has a heart attack on the job. Keith found him and called 911. He was doing CPR when the ambulance came; it was too late, though. Still, everyone in town thinks the guy's a real hero, so when he ran for the town board position, it was unopposed. Crazy, huh?"

"I guess it's only fair that he keeps tabs on where you're living, given that you know everything there is to know about him," Grady said.

"He keeps tabs on me *because* he knows I know everything about him."

"My firm has been handling the multiple suits against Veteran Renewal for going on ten years now. I've been working on those cases since I've been out of law school."

"What cases? They weren't insulating homes with toxic fertilizer were they?"

Susan chuckled, her humor back again. "As a

matter of fact, and this is common knowledge, so I'm not breaking any laws here by telling you this…" Still, Susan lowered her voice. "Veteran Renewal made a practice of inflating the price for building materials. Then, after taking the money from developers, built houses on the cheap. It's how they made out so well. The case I'm working on now claims that they knowingly pumped illegal asbestos insulation into about half the attics of those hastily built homes in Eden Heights."

"No shit."

"A couple of folks came down with cancer, and they're looking for someone to blame." Susan shook her head at the reality of it. "If Glen hadn't died, chances are the blame would have settled on his shoulders. As it is, we're looking for the guys he worked with—but they've scattered all over the place."

"What about the developers who sold the contracts to Clelland?" Grady asked.

"It's the Clellands' fault because they installed the stuff without the developers knowing. They skimped on supplies and still charged the regular price. That's how they got so rich."

"So is Keith going down instead?"

"That's just it," Susan said, shaking her head. "Keith comes off clean because he just joined the business after he got back from the war. They were in the development side of it by then. But I know the Clellands; they're a bad lot, war medals or not. That's why I'm so suspicious of this whole Glenwoods Development plan."

"Wait, they're going to tear down Worthingdale Woods and put up the Glenwoods Development?" Grady asked in disgust.

"Yeah, that's the deal. But screw him, right?"

"Right," Grady said.

Then, raising her glass, she tilted it toward him and said, "Here's to old friends, anyway. There's probably better stuff for us to talk about."

"Cheers."

She swallowed a gulp of ale and said, "By the way, I'm sorry I slapped you all those years ago."

"It hurt, you know."

"You still remember?"

"Hell yes. You should know I felt guilty about that for years."

"Years?"

"Well, maybe not years, but for a long time."

"Wow, I didn't know I had that sort of power over boys."

"It wasn't the slap so much, Susan, but more what you said."

"God... all I remember is that you were drunk and all over me, and then I let you have it."

"But when you told me you 'thought I was a good guy'... I don't know, the past tense just killed me."

She laughed. "Well, what happened to pull you back from the abyss of douche-baggery?"

Grady took a long pull from his glass, cleared his throat, and said, "This girl I met, Briarly. It was mostly her who saved me."

"Oh," Susan said, a little too quickly. "I didn't know there was a Briarly. That you had found someone, I mean."

"Yeah, I did."

"What happened? I mean, not that it's my business or anything."

"Jesus, you really are a lawyer aren't you?" She laughed and leaned toward him. Grady took a drink and said, "Next question, counselor."

"Where is she now?"

"Massachusetts."

"Massachusetts? And you're back here?"

"Yeah. I'm back here. For now anyway." He swallowed his words and looked past her in silence before finishing off his beer.

"But she saved you, huh?"

"Yeah, you could say that. The slap helped too

though. I owe you for that."

"How about you get the next pitcher, and we'll call it even."

"Fair enough."

Silence fell between them. After a couple of minutes Susan said, "I'll be right back," grabbed her purse and walked toward the back of the bar. She disappeared through the crowd toward the bathroom. Grady poured himself another drink.

Grady was well into his third beer when he began to feel self-conscious sitting alone as the Friday night crowd thickened around him. He turned in his chair to look toward the ladies' room, where he assumed Susan went to freshen up, and as he did, he saw Keith Clelland staggering toward him with an empty glass in his hand.

Clelland slid into Susan's seat and slurred at Grady, "You owe me a beer." Then he poured himself a full pint, drank it halfway down, and then poured what was left in the pitcher into his glass.

"Looks like the little lady left you all alone, teacher man."

"She'll be back," Grady said. "Look, Keith. I'm sorry... "

"You know when I saw that my boy Seamus had you in class, I knew it'd be trouble."

"What do you mean?"

"I heard about you. People talk. Brothers talk is what I mean. Guess I thought an arrogant prick like you… probably hold shit against my kid."

Grady looked back over his shoulder again to see if he could find Susan in the crowd.

"She left, asshole. You think I'm kidding?"

"She'll be back."

"Jesus, what do you want to hit that for anyway?" Clelland snorted. "Tired old lawyer bitch, doesn't know when to shut her fucking mouth."

"I guess you and she have a lot in common then," Grady said. It took a beat for Clelland to recognize he'd been insulted.

"Listen, teacher man," he said, downing the rest of the beer in front of him. "You may think you own this town, but I've got news for you. You aren't shit here compared to me, so you better get the fuck out. Who knows what might happen to you otherwise."

For a moment Grady considered his options, and then he remembered two things: Keith Clelland was a soldier who was trained to kill people, and Susan Luster, who looked damn good tonight, was in the ladies' room. "Are you threatening me, Keith? Because it certainly wouldn't look good for the police to get a harassment call concerning a member of the town board whose company also just happens to be starting a major construction project on the other side of town. I might not be a big shit like you, but I'll bet that somebody might think twice about pulling the lever in your favor if they knew you were hanging out at The Well threatening a guy who'd just given you a beer."

"You didn't give me that beer," he said flatly. "Now, before I go, I want to tell you why I came over here. Unless you got something else you wanna say?" Grady waited. "You stay the fuck away from my boy. I hear you're giving him shit, and you'll answer to me. I ain't joking."

"I'm his teacher, Keith. How am I supposed to stay away from him?"

"And that goes for my business as well. And that goes for your little girlfriend too." Grady was silent. "I got plans. You hear me?" Clelland asked. Grady nodded. "Good. I won't say it again." As Clelland stood, his legs caught the table and sent Grady's half-full beer tumbling unto his lap, the empty pitcher skittering across the floor. "Oops," Keith smiled. "Sorry, teacher man."

Grady sat for a moment, watching the man stumble back to the bar. It was clear Clelland was right: Susan was gone. If there was a back door to the place, she must have used it, but there would be time to solve that mystery. For now, Grady bent over and picked up the pitcher from the floor. He used his sleeve to wipe the beer, which had pooled on the ledge of the table back toward the middle where Susan's empty glass lay toppled on its side. His pants were soaked, but he knew, even though the bar seemed suddenly packed with people, that the lights were low and he would have no problem leaving without drawing much attention to himself.

As Grady walked out the door, he looked back to see that Keith Clelland had ordered himself another pitcher and was once again pouring himself a glass of beer. Sitting next to him at the bar was Grady's brother, Emile.

Ward Gregory's apartment hardly looked like the same place. The landlord had replaced the stained ceiling tiles, fixed the toilet, and cleaned the floors and appliances so efficiently that they almost looked new. It was late, but seemed much later by the time Grady showered again and made up his bed for his first night's sleep in his new place. Before he lay down, Grady opened the window to let the early autumn air filter in. It was more than an hour before he fell asleep.

Late in the night he woke to the sound of garbled voices, then as if with a switch, they fell silent. A moment later a sensation rushed over him. Suddenly he was in water. Looking up, he saw swirls above him and tried to pull himself up toward the surface, but the current pushed him back down. He was gasping as though breathing through a wet cloth.

Then he saw himself clearly in the shadows of the gully in the woods. The sun framing the silhouettes of the trees. He heard cries coming from the highest branches as he searched the shattered sky for light. He was kneeling. One hand on the blood-soaked earth. The turkey vultures slowly circling overhead.

It was night again. The blue light of the moon reflected in the eyes of the deer that surrounded him. Their breath froze in the air as clouds before them. Their bodies were frail. Their fur, threadbare. He inhaled deeply through his nose. The deer shook their heads in recognition of the sounds of life. Their jittery stick legs carried them to the outskirts of the trees.

He looked after them into the darkness and saw an emerging figure stumble toward him. A fawn. Its wasted siblings folded themselves back into the silence of the woods, and Grady was left alone in the clearing with only the night and the yearling for company. Above he heard sharp cries and looking up, saw that the sky was thick with blackbirds. He was certain they were calling for him.

Nothing Here is Real

Grady's eyes opened and searched the semi-darkness for something he could recognize. Was he awake? He felt the bed shift beneath him. He slid his feet to the floor. "I'm awake," he said in the darkness. Still, he heard the blackbirds cawing into the night. He walked across the room and put his head out the window for a breath of air.

In the half-light of dawn he saw the branches of the nearby cedar trees boiling with sleek, black bodies. Blackbirds. The trees were alive with their movements. Grady slammed the window shut and stumbled back into the room. His breath was gone. His shirt was wet with sweat. He climbed back into bed, and pulling his knees to his chest, he wrapped his arms over his head and waited for the end.

WATER WAR

Although my mother thought Sandy
Fussell was nice enough, she never
approved of my brother's interest in her
daughter, Mary. "You can do better than
that girl, Emile, let me tell you that.
She takes after her father in almost
every way. If you ask me, the whole
family would be better off if she were
to have gone and lived with the man like
she wanted to. Can you imagine the nerve
of that child, Frank?"

My father had just walked in the
door from work after pulling a rare
overnight shift at the group home. He had
no idea Dan Fussell, the man who stood to

my father's right as they sang together
every Sunday in the church choir, had
finally come clean and admitted to his
wife and children he was seeing Tammy
Seibold on the side.

"After all that her mother's done
for her, she up and sides with her
father. He was the one who cheated, for
God's sake." My father was accustomed to
walking into the buzz saw of my mother's
righteous indignation and nodded his
head in agreement. He lifted an eyebrow
of a hello to my brother and me.

"Did Sandy call?" my father asked.

"I told her if she ever needed
to stay here for any reason, she was
more than welcome to. Imagine that
man running off with Tammy Seibold
of all people." My father rubbed his
forehead thoughtfully. Sensing that the
conversation had taken an adult turn,
Emile and I slunk out of the room.

The Fussells' impending divorce
became something of a sensation around

our dinner table. For weeks Sandy
continued filling my mother's ears with
stories of her failed marriage. Never one
to keep her opinions to herself, my mother
proceeded to report back to my father,
with mounting disgust, the gory details
of Dan Fussell's infidelity. On more
than one occasion a good twenty minutes
of retelling took place before my mother
realized that my brother and I were still
at the dinner table listening with open
mouths.

What my parents didn't know
is that I was getting an almost daily
dose of another side of the story from
Allen Fussell, who apparently assumed
I was interested in hearing about the
deconstruction of his family. He'd corner
me in the hallway or slide up next to me
in the cafeteria and tell me the latest
from home. Allen knew Emile loved his
sister, and must have thought that I,
in turn, would treasure any inside
information I could get on her to hold
over Emile's head.

Nothing Here is Real

The little knowledge Emile had of
the sexually deviant behavior of Mary
Fussell's father seemed to inspire him
to new heights of admiration for her.
Shortly after Sandy Fussell's initial
call to our house, my brother began
calling Mary every night before he went
to bed. Sandy saw the calls as "sweet".
Mary saw the calls as the beginning
stages of stalking, which of course is
why she protested so sincerely the notion
of inviting Emile to her Halloween party.
Boys like Emile Pickett were not to be
encouraged.

The way Allen told it, the deal
Mary and his mother came to was simple:
she wouldn't move in with her father, who
took an apartment over the ice cream shop
on Water Street, if her mother permitted
her to have a sleepover Halloween party.
When Mary first proposed the idea to
Sandy, it was a great relief to her
mother. Hosting a Halloween party for a
handful of fourteen-year-old girls the

day before the kids came begging for candy seemed worth the trouble, if it meant her baby girl would be willing to stay under her roof while the separation from Dan ran its course. But when Mary mentioned that she wanted to invite boys, well then, things changed for Sandy.

The thought of her basement full of girls in bras and boys with their little peckers swelling in their pants playing spin the bottle was just too much for Sandy to bear. "That's where I draw the line, sweetheart. You can invite anyone you want, so long as they sit down to go pee. And no sleepovers. I can't handle that right now."

"Mom, this is bullshit." Mary's new habit of swearing in front of her mother was another ancillary benefit of spending more "quality time" with her dad. "These girls, the ones I want to invite, they won't come if boys aren't invited."

"Let me think about it," Sandy said, in reply.

Nothing Here is Real

"Fine, I've got to pack a few things up to take back to Dad's anyway," Mary said, keeping her mother's feet to the fire. "Let me know where I'll be living, when you've made up your mind."

I was eating breakfast in the other room when I overheard my mother's side of a phone conversation with Sandy. My mother must have thought I was outside helping my dad and Emile with yard work, because she lay on her bed with the door to her room open and spoke freely of Mary's latest stunt. What I gathered from my mother's end of the conversation was that Sandy, desperate to have her daughter out of the clutches of her husband, was leaning toward agreeing. My mother listened with both hands wrapped around the phone. When she spoke she became animated.

"Sandy, if you agree without limitations, you're setting yourself up for a hell-ride down the road...

"Well, you could give it a theme...

"I don't know, something that would keep the kids decent, but at the same time, it's got to be something they wouldn't think you thought up for that reason. Does Mary have a costume yet? You could think of something for her...

"You think she'd do that, wear something revealing just to get under your skin? My God, I'm glad I have boys," my mother cackled. "No, they could always take that too far. How about the circus? Circus costumes aren't racy...

"That's true. Okay, so say she wants to be a trapeze girl or something. Just get her a leotard to wear. A leotard is nothing more than a bathing suit really. I think that's as good as you're going to get, Sandy. Besides, she's a fourteen-year-old girl. If she wants to show off her boobs and dance around boys, she'll think you letting her wear a leotard is perfect. Trust me.

"I totally get that. I would be worried about what's going on as well. Couldn't you just insist on being down there? It's your house...

"You really think it's that big of
a deal that she'd want to call the whole
thing off if you suggested it?"

I could see out of the corner of
my eye that my mother was now sitting
up on her bed facing the mirror above
her dresser. She was moving her hands
with exaggerated animation as she spoke.
Every so often she would toss her hair
away from her eyes. "Okay, Sandy, I've got
an idea about what we can do if you're
worried about what'll go on when you're
not around. Why not have Mary invite
Emile? I know the two of them have been
talking a lot ever since you and Dan
split. I think Emile is very concerned
about her.

"It solves the problem because
Emile tells me everything. I mean ev-
ery-thing, Sandy. It's like he's still my
little buddy. Just the other day when I
was putting him to bed, he told me that
this bad case of acne he's gotten lately
is really making him shy around girls.

I noticed there were all of these blotchy patches of blood on his pillow. He told me--and get this, he made me promise I wouldn't tell Frank--that he uses the sharp end of Frank's beard trimming scissors to lop off the tops of his zits. He said, in all seriousness, he thinks-I'm quoting here--'If you've got to have zits, girls like them when they're freshly squeezed.' Can you believe it? He tells me everything.

"Right. I'll just ask Emile. Better yet, I'll give him a big pep talk before he goes and tell him to keep on eye out for Mary. She's vulnerable; he'll eat that up. I love the kid, don't get me wrong, but he knows next to nothing about girls. Like this: last summer I forgot to flush one night when I had my period, and I guess when he went to pee in the middle of the night he saw the bloody water and just freaked out. He woke me up, almost in tears. He was super embarrassed after I explained it, even made me promise not to tell Grady. So you see what I'm saying about him not knowing the first thing about girls. I'm sure if I prime him right, he'll be a good little watchdog for you.

"Oh, sure thing. I'm glad I could help.

"Okay then, Sandy. Let me know how it goes. Good luck."

I was asleep when my father brought my brother home. I waited an hour while my brother and then my father and mother washed up. When I was sure the light in the hall was out and that my parents were in bed, I crept out of my room and up the hall to Emile's closed door, hoping to ask him about the party. I grasped the doorknob and pushed lightly to find the door wasn't latched. I held my breath, waiting to see if my movements had woken my brother. In my breathless silence, I heard a murmuring coming from inside the room: two distinct voices playing off of each other in an easy give and take of information. I pushed the door open

a crack. My brother's nightlight lit
the room enough for me to see my mother
sitting on the edge of Emile's bed. He lay
on his back, with his knees bent, telling
her the story of his first kiss.

Mary Fussell was dressed in a skin-
tight, pink and black leotard. Her hair
was pulled up in a bun, and she was
wearing make-up, lots of it. Emile said
the combination of the make-up and the
outfit made her look like a woman twice
her age. Every boy noticed.

After everyone was pretty sure no
parents were going to come down, Mary
got behind the little bar her father set
up in the corner of the basement and
produced a near empty bottle of whiskey.
She told everyone, now that her dad lived
uptown, no one checked the contents of
the bottles anymore; she opened it and
downed the final swig. Everybody just
watched her. She directed them to sit
down in a circle, then she put the empty
whiskey bottle in the middle and pointed
at Lisa Fanneck to start the game.

Nothing Here is Real

The rules were simple. After the
spinning bottle came to a rest, you and
the person the mouth of the bottle was
pointing at got up in the middle of
the circle and kissed--no cheek kisses
allowed; they had to be on the lips. If
the bottle pointed to someone who was
your same sex you were off the hook.
Mary announced they would go around the
circle two full times. The first round
would be lip kisses, and the second round
would be French kisses.

Emile said everyone seemed excited
at first--kind of nervous and excited
at the same time. But when it came to
spinning the bottle, none of the girls
seemed to want to do it. Finally, Lisa
spun it, but it came to rest on Mandy
Hiller, so she didn't have to kiss
anybody. It looked like the whole thing
was going to break up when Kenny Holmes
stepped into the circle and came up with
a plan. Only the boys would spin the
bottle.

The ratio of girls to boys was about

two to one, so Kenny's plan was likely
to give most of the girls an out. Emile
said every guy was hating Kenny, until
he suggested a new rule: they'd only go
around the circle once, but before every
guy spun the bottle, the girl next to him
would pick what would end up happening-
kiss on the lips, French kiss or. . .spend
seven minutes in heaven.

Emile explained to my captivated
mother that seven minutes in heaven
meant the couple would be locked in a
closet, with the lights off, for seven
minutes-enough time to presumably do
whatever you pleased.

The game was pretty uneventful,
Emile said. All of the girls were playing
it safe, until Emile came up to spin. Lisa
Fanneck was sitting next to Emile, and
when it was his turn, she handed him
the bottle and raised the ante. "Seven
minutes in heaven," she said.

My mother listened silently to most
of this, only interrupting my brother to
ask brief questions of clarification. Who

is this Kenny Holmes? (A boy who, like
Mary, had been in Emile's classes since
he was a kid.) How did you know it was
whiskey in the bottle? (Mary had called
it "Turkey Juice" because of the bird
on the label.) Are Lisa and Mary good
friends? (They're always together, but
most people think they secretly hate each
other.)

Now that the story seemed to be
reaching its climax, my mother shifted
down in the bed to give Emile room to sit
up.

Mary jumped up when Emile's spin
came to a rest on her and took his hand.
She led him to the closet in the corner.

"Did the two of you turn on the
lights?" I heard my mother ask.

"No, we didn't really have to. After
we were inside for about thirty seconds
we could see each other. That's when she
started to kiss me."

"She kissed you?"

"Yeah, like you wouldn't believe."

"Did it feel nice to have her kiss

you?"

"I was a little overwhelmed because she was really into it. All the other kids were outside of the door, counting down the time every thirty seconds."

"What were you doing?" My mother was speaking softly, so I had to strain to hear all of the words.

"I was kissing her back."

"Where were your hands?"

"Well, I was holding onto the door handle with one. I didn't want anyone to open it. But Mary grabbed my wrist and put my hands on her waist. The more we kissed the more I moved them all around."

"Did you go up her shirt?" My shock at the boldness of my mother's questions was only trumped by the ease with which Emile answered them.

"Remember, she was wearing a leotard, Mom. We just touched each other outside of our clothes."

"She touched you?"

"Yes."

"I see. Then what happened?"

Nothing Here is Real

"The door opened, and we kind of
fell out onto the ground, because we had
been leaning against the door. Everybody
thought that was really funny. Kenny
Holmes was pissed, though, because he
likes Mary, but what can you do? I felt
bad for the guy."

"Are you and Mary an item now?"

"I'm not sure. We really didn't talk
the rest of the party. Dad was the first
parent to show up."

"Did you tell her you'd call her or
anything?"

"I didn't have a chance. She was
hanging with her girlfriends the rest
of the night. The game broke up after we
were in the closet."

My mother's tone turned serious. "I
really think, Emile, if you are going to
allow a girl to touch you like that, even
a fast girl like Mary Fussell, you owe it
to yourself, and to me, to at least try to
make her your girlfriend. You're not just
a piece of meat."

My brother, who had shifted his

position at the onset of the closet story
so he was sitting cross-legged, facing my
mother, suddenly lurched forward and
threw his arms around her neck.

"You know you don't have to worry
about me, Mom," he said. "I know what I'm
doing."

"Well," my mother sighed, "I should
certainly hope so."

I was jerked out of my stunned
state when my mother abruptly reached up
and pulled the chain of the light that
hung above Emile's bed. Instantly the
room was illuminated. They would have
seen me had I not had the presence of
mind to crab-walk back down the hallway,
leaving the door slightly ajar. But, in
that moment of hurried clarity, as I
blinked away the blindness of the lamp's
sudden light, I saw my mother, with her
hand on his head, easing Emile back into
a horizontal position as she cooed, "Now
let's take a look at those blackheads
before you go to sleep."

Nothing Here is Real

On the condition that every student participate, our teachers agreed to give up a day of traditional instruction so the students could fully enjoy Halloween through a series of themed events--skits, a costume contest, and a professional acting troupe's rendition of Edgar Allan Poe's "The Raven." Full participation meant, among other things, that everyone was required to wear his costume for the entire day.

On Halloween morning, I was greeted by an oversized shirt-box sitting at my place at the table. In it I found the costume my mom had put together for me to wear to school that day.

From the box I unfolded black tights, a black turtleneck, white gloves, a shining pair of new white Keds, and what looked like a hat of some kind. I was instructed to go into the bathroom and try it on. After I was dressed, I called to my mother, "Mom, I think it's kinda tight."

She came into the bathroom and

smiled, "That's how it's supposed to look, Grady." Then she painted red circles on my cheeks and drew quick lines around my mouth and eyes with a tube of her old lipstick. "There," she said. "I've never seen a more convincing mime."

"Mom, I can't... "

As I began to register my objection to the costume, my father walked into the bathroom.

"Wow, Grady!" he said. "Your mother sure did a great job of putting that together for you, didn't she?" I could see in his posture he was ready to pounce if I so much as stuttered a word of contempt for the work she had done to outfit me.

"You can't what?" my mother said, ignoring my father's implicit compliment.

"I can't say I disagree with you, Mom," I smiled into the mirror. "I've never seen a more convincing mime, either."

That day in school, in between every period, my stylishly outfitted classmates cackled and chided me, hurling insults

and accusations about my manhood as I
squeaked up the hallways in my new white
shoes. The treatment I received from
teachers was worse. They would size up my
outfit, taking me in from head-to-toe, and
then, while trying to suppress laughter,
ignore me completely, so as to not fall in
with my classmates' open mockery of my
appearance.

Lunch was by far the worst
period of the day. Early in the period
Jim Robinson hurled a half-full milk
carton at me that missed my chair by
inches. When I retaliated by chucking
my blueberry cobbler at his head, I
was banished to the front table of the
cafeteria, at once alone and on full
display. Every eye in the room was turned
on me to comic effect. Girls in tight-
fitting cat outfits laughed at me. Boys in
biker gear called me a pussy, but the most
insulting of all the degradations came
from Allen Fussell, who, five minutes
before the end of the period, snuck up
behind me, placed his hands on the back

of his head so that he looked like he was preparing to do some kind of vertical sit-up, and began thrusting his hips forward and back in an obscene gesture, the meaning of which was instantly grasped by all: my juvenile mime-boy outfit and made-up face were all the proof anyone needed that my heart's deepest desire was to have someone fuck me up the ass.

I turned around just in time to see his final thrust. My eyes met his as the bell rang, and simultaneously the rest of the cafeteria rose in an impromptu standing ovation for Allen's perfectly timed performance.

"You're an asshole, Allen," I said. "I thought we were friends."

"Not after the shit your brother pulled at my house Saturday night we're not."

"What are you talking about?"

"The Halloween party," he said, as if it needed no more explanation. "Your brother's a loser."

To my surprise, an urge to defend

Emile rose in my chest. "Why is it Emile's fault your sister's a slutty whore?"

"First of all," he said, growing red in the face, "don't talk about my sister like that. This has nothing to do with her. It was your brother who messed everything up by starting the fight in the basement. If he hadn't ratted everyone out to my mother, she would never have called everyone's parents. Mary is so pissed at my mom that she's talking about moving back in with my dad again. So no, we're not friends anymore, Grady."

The room had cleared by that point, but for some reason the cafeteria aides ignored Allen and me, as we stood facing each other in front of the room, truant and arguing over our families.

"Your sister took my brother in a closet and essentially raped him. I heard him telling my mom the story the other night."

"I don't care what your brother said to your mom." Allen was wide-eyed

in defense of his family. "But facts are
your brother and Kenny Holmes got into a
pushing match that Mary had to break up.
My mother went down there when she heard
all of the slamming around and pulled
Emile upstairs." I shook my head in
disbelief. "I know that's what happened,"
Allen countered. "I was sitting in the
living room listening to it, Grady. My
mother told him she was going to have
to take him home. That's when he started
ratting everyone out--telling her how
Kenny had snuck in a bottle of whiskey
from home and how Kenny and Mary were
in the closet getting it on. He told her
everything. My mother just flipped.

"How come my parents don't know any
of this?" I asked.

"All my mom told them was that the
party was over, same as the other parents.
She knows what everyone in town thinks
about our house; she's not going to make it
worse by telling everyone everything."

"I don't believe you," I said.
"Emile's story was totally different."

"Well, Emile is full of shit, mime-boy."

"Why would he lie? He told me that it was your sister who drank the booze out of your dad's bar."

"There's no bar in our basement."

"And that it was her and Emile going at it in the closet."

"My sister wouldn't touch your brother if he were the last guy on Earth. My mother made her invite him. They had a huge fight about it, but it was one of the conditions my mom insisted upon. She did it out of pity. Everyone knows what a loser your brother is, how he doesn't have any friends."

My lunch rose in my throat. Without saying another word, I turned on my sparkling white heels and stormed back to class.

Allen Fussell must have told his sister Emile's version of the party because the next day in gym class Kenny Holmes decked Emile as he went up for a lay-up, sending him sprawling and evoking a chorus of laughter from the other players on the court. When Emile publicly protested the rough treatment, Kenny challenged him to a fight after school. Had the challenge been made in the privacy of a stairwell or some other dark corner of the school free of witnesses, it could have been shaken off as bravado--but it wasn't. Half of Mr. Popper's fifth-period gym class heard the challenge and just as many, if not more, of their peers heard Emile's willing acceptance of it. They would meet in the back corner of the graveyard, looking over the ravine, three o'clock sharp.

I heard about the "high school fight" as I walked home. No one knew who it was going to be between, but that didn't really matter. These kinds of gatherings were fairly common in Apollo. We'd meet at a designated place and watch the exchange of blows, then retire to our respective cliques to recount the events as if we were ringside reporters. No one

ever really got hurt--just black eyes
and bloody noses. What we didn't know as
we made our way through the tombstones
that day was Kenny Holmes had something
different in mind.

As my peers and I approached the
back corner of the graveyard, we could
see a small group already gathered. The
usual crowd was there: guys who smoked
cigarettes and grew their hair long in
the back. They loved this kind of thing
and always rooted for bloodshed, but as
my friends and I got closer to the crowd,
and the participants came into sharper
focus, we saw something truly shocking:
the rabble wasn't just made up of guys;
there were girls there as well, the type
of girls we never saw in middle school--
girls with tits and make-up.
The girls were standing together,
ringed by a group of would-be thugs in
black concert T-shirts, who spoke in low
tones and spit after every sentence as a
point of emphasis. My group stopped ten

yards from the intersection of the two
dirt paths that bisected the cemetery
where the fight was to take place. To
a middle schooler's mind, this was the
ideal position to watch a fight: close
enough to see almost everything and far
enough away to make a quick escape if the
cops arrived to break things up. It wasn't
until I had settled into my seat on top of
the granite memorial of William B. Haynes
(born August 5, 1908; received into heaven
September 23, 1969) that I recognized the
girl in the middle group as Mary Fussell.
Then I saw Emile.

I was so busy trying to decide
whether or not I should go and stand
behind my brother that I hadn't noticed
Kenny Holmes, walking shoulder to
shoulder with a handful of henchmen,
as he approached the crowd. The rise of
a collective murmur and a spattering
of cheers shook me out of my daze, and I
looked up in time to see the spectators
part so Kenny could get through to meet
my brother.

Nothing Here is Real

Emile caught the first punch fully on the jaw. It snapped his head back violently in a way that seemed both unnatural and painfully real. The momentum of the blow carried Emile back a few steps and then his body crumpled to the ground. Kenny was on top of him in an instant.

All of the kids were cheering now, yelling terrible things, crying for more. Kenny pulled my brother's shirt over his head and was blindly pumping his fists into the mass of arms and fabric and skull. Emile tried to pull his legs to his head to protect himself, but he was unable to fully shelter his body from the blows.

Kenny rolled Emile over on to his back and straddled his chest, pinning my brother on his back. He reached down with both hands and tore Emile's shirt from his body. From where I sat, I could see the buttons flying off in crazy directions. Emile lay half-naked and lifeless on the ground.

It was this indecency that seemed
to wake Emile, and he began to thrash
in an attempt to throw Kenny off, but
leverage and weight were on Kenny's
side. Then Kenny placed his right hand
on Emile's neck and pinned his head
sideways in the dirt. That was the first
time I saw my brother's eyes.

Emile's face was scarlet and swollen
with the strain of his entrapment. His
eyes and mouth were open with the effort
of his escape. He was kicking his legs
wildly, but with Kenny's full weight on
his chest and his own head pinned in the
dirt at such an awkward angle, there was
really nothing my brother could do but
lie there and wait for the next blow to
fall. Kenny seemed to sense his advantage
and paused, so the crowd of my brother's
peers could fully take in how thoroughly
he had been beaten.

Without really knowing it, I had
left my post on the gravestone and
advanced toward the crowd. I now stood
in full view of the ring of taunting

teenagers, in the same spot where my
brother stood before the first blow felled
him. There was a maddening collection
of indistinguishable sounds--hurried
voices, clapping, and shouts, but I heard
none of it directly. It was as if all my
senses save sight were muted.

"Hey, motherfucker?"

I looked up, aware for the first
time that Kenny was now addressing me.
"What do you think of your big brother
now, huh?" he asked. Then he cleared his
throat and dropped a long wet string of
spit into Emile's ear.

"Stop," I said. "That's enough."

"Not yet," he said, shaking his head
in exaggerated denial.

He reached his left hand into his
mouth to produce an oozing wad of pig-
pink gum. He briefly held it in the air
so everyone could grasp what it was he
was about to do. Then he plunged the gum
into my brother's hair. He churned and
twisted it until it was lost in a sea of
strawberry blonde knots on my brother's

head. It was only then that Emile began
to cry--to wail really, in low dirt-choked
sobs. "Get off me. Get the fuck off me, you
bastard!"

"What's that, Emile? You still
talking?" Kenny taunted. But even the
crowd of classmates fell silent once they
saw the gum in my brother's hair.

Sensing that with Emile's tears the
fight was now over, Kenny jumped to his
feet. He took me in with a long slow gaze,
and then shook his head. With the weight
of his classmate off him, Emile, shirtless
and shamed, curled into a fetal ball and
rocked in the dust and broken stone of
the cemetery path, sobbing and cursing.
"Take a good look," Kenny said, pointing
at the huddled mass on the ground that
was my brother. "That right there is a
lying piece of shit."

"That's about enough, don't you
think?" It was the voice of a man, a man
no one noticed coming up the path.

Kenny looked up and without a
second thought sprinted toward the

ravine. The rest of the crowd, girls and guys alike, scattered with a similar urgency, as if somehow their jeering presence in the crowd made them equally guilty of the cruel violence Kenny Holmes had perpetrated on Emile.

The silence of the afternoon rushed back in to fill the void left by the violent swirl of the departed witnesses. Emile's sobs seemed louder now, as the man and I stood looking at each other.

"Go ahead," the man said. "Get the hell out of here."

I looked down at Emile, writhing in the dust, just now seeming to fully realize the magnitude of his pain. "That's my brother," I said, pointing to Emile.

"It's a little late for that, don't you think?" the man said, stepping into the clearing. "I live right over there." He threw his head over his shoulder in acknowledgment of where he had come from. "It looks like your brother might need some help. I'll see he gets home."

"But..."

The man raised his right arm and
pointed over my shoulder at the dusty
graveside road.

"It's time for you to go," he said. I
waited a beat looking first at my silent
brother and then at the man who came
to his rescue. Then I walked out of the
cemetery, leaving Emile in the hands of a
stranger.

When I got home, an hour later, my
mother was there. The light was on in
the bathroom. I could hear voices coming
from the half-opened door. "Don't move,
honey. I'll be able to get it out sooner if
you don't move." She was standing behind
Emile, holding a melting ice cube in her
left hand, while systematically applying
it to bunches of my brother's hair. After
pulling her left hand back, she used her
right hand to pull pieces of my brother's
hair out of the stiffened gum. I could
see the pink, stringing clumps of gum as
my mother pulled the mass apart with her
thumb and middle finger. My brother's

legs were spread and his hands were on
the bathroom counter. I gathered from
the small clumps of hair that littered
Emile's shoulders that my mother had
initially thought to cut the gum out, but
had given up in the face of the seemingly
impossible task. Emile's hair was in
knots.

My brother was crying softly. His
mouth was open, and his eyes were closed.
His face was wet with tears. His lips
seemed thinner to me than they ever had.
His teeth were showing, and there was
a line of spit connecting his upper and
lower gums. The sound of his growing
anguish seemed to come from his hips. It
was low and deep, but at the same time
airy. It sounded like a slow wind blowing
through an untethered sail.

"I'm not going to be able to get
it out, Emile," my mother said, plainly
raising the back of her right hand to her
forehead. She looked up in the mirror and
only then realized I was standing in the
doorway watching them. "You watched?" she

asked. Then, without saying another word, she shut the door.

I stood in the corner of the kitchen as she scribbled a note to my father and, pulling Emile by the elbow, slammed out of the house. I couldn't bring myself to read her message. I was afraid they had left forever.

My father came home from work and read my mother's note. He walked into the living room where I sat, watching for his reaction and said, "It looks like it's just you and me, Bud." My heart sank. They had left.

"What?" I sputtered, on the brink of tears.

"Mom left a note that said she took Emile to get a haircut and then out to get a bite to eat. She said you didn't want to go, so I should just make something up here." Then, noticing my reaction, my father paused. "Is something going on?" It was on the tip of my tongue to tell him what happened, but where would I begin?

Nothing Here is Real

When she returned that evening
with a freshly-sheared Emile in tow and
explained to my father what happened--
how she had come home to find Emile
bruised and soaking in a bath--she gave
my father three options: drive over to
the Holmes' house, pull that little son-
of-a-bitch outside, and kick his ass;
start taking a more active interest in
the lives of her boys; or divorce her,
so she could find a man who would. My
father, who was used to shouldering
the brunt of all facets of my mother's
frustration, listened patiently. Then he
suggested rather than responding with
violence to the violent act of a clearly
disturbed boy, perhaps what Emile really
needed was a positive outlet for his
energy, something that would give him
the confidence he needed to walk away
when challenged to a fight knowing, as
my father put it, "The strength of a man
lies not in his ability to destroy, but in
his ability to create." My mother, who was

still hot for revenge three hours after
hearing the story for the first time,
took some convincing, but in the end she
agreed to let my father try it his way.

The Boy Scouts had taught my father
the skills he needed to stand on his
own. To be trustworthy, loyal, helpful,
friendly, courteous, and kind. The Boy
Scouts had taught him how to live off the
land, respect its people, and honor his
own limitations. But most importantly,
the Boy Scouts had saved my father from
having to fight.

It was 1968. Everything was
changing. Many of Eden Height's boys
had already been drafted. In a series
of brutal weeks that spring, the bodies
of six of them were sent home. The ugly
truth, as my father saw it, was this war
made no sense. People were dying for
ideas that had no foothold in the world
my father was coming to know. Still, he
deeply believed in his country and knew,
come February, he would fill out his

paperwork with the Selective Service and leave his fate to God. He fully expected his number would be called--"felt the itch of it in his toes," is how he always explained it.

Having finished the required merit badge work the past spring, my father spent the summer before he turned eighteen organizing his Eagle Scout project. It was approved and in the end would lead to his receiving his just rank, but to my dad, what he was trying to do went way beyond Boy Scouts.

On the surface, it was simply a beautification project. He and the rest of the boys of the troop were to cut the wood, assemble, and then distribute, for display on the historic Main Street of Eden Heights, twenty ornate flower boxes. My father worked with the ladies of the garden club to secure the flowers and was able to convince the men at Emmanuel's Hardware to donate the wood, stain, and nails required for the task. It was my father's job to design the boxes and oversee the boys' construction of them.

To my dad's mind, symbolically speaking, it was a perfect project for the times. It brought together elements of the fragmented community in the name of reclaiming a sense of beauty for the town. When the V.F.W. post got wind of the project and offered to donate twenty miniature American flags, my father thought, why not? It's a beautiful country, war or no war.

The boys were gathered in the basement of the church, the ladies from the garden club had the flowers all set out and ready for pick up, and the bags of potting soil were stacked neatly in the parking lot ready to be poured when my father slipped. In his hand was a table saw. He was using it to demonstrate to the younger boys how the floor pieces of the flower boxes were to be cut. In a bloody instant, he separated his trigger finger from the rest of his right hand.

The troop leaders sprung into action. A tourniquet was applied to

the stump and a young boy from Apollo
policed up the finger. But even though
the severed digit was wrapped in a
handful of ice from the church's cooler of
lemonade, the nature of the cut made it
impossible to reattach. The war was over
for my father.

My dad took Emile's shaved head and
bruised face as the world's declaration
of war on his eldest son; Emile was being
called to fight. Given his own past when
faced with a similar plight, my dad
naturally thought of Boy Scouts as a way
of saving Emile. We joined Troop 637 the
next day.

Bob Gerehart was a sergeant
major in Vietnam. He served three tours
of duty-volunteered for each one. He
believed in the United States of America.
He believed in the cause. He wanted to
go kill some Commies, and he did. He was
Apollo's most decorated solider. He had
walked at the front of every Fourth of

July parade since coming back home. When
the hippies protested, he personally
kicked their asses. He was often asked to
speak at the graveside services of fallen
servicemen, and when he did, he always
spoke of the honor of service, the call to
duty, the beauty of military order and
how it stood in stark contrast to the ways
of the rest of the world. So even though
he didn't have any sons of his own, Bob
Gerehart wanted to be involved in Boy
Scouts because, to his mind, scouting
stood for everything that had once been
right in the world, and could be again,
so help him God.

Of course, I knew none of this the
first time I saw Bob Gerehart in the
basement of Creekside United Methodist
church, wearing his neatly pressed tan
scout shirt and leading the troop in the
pledge to the flag. All I knew then was
he was the man from the graveyard, the
man who had broken up the fight--Emile's
savior.

Nothing Here is Real

The spring canoe trip was a
tradition in Troop 637. The boys and their
dads would drop their canoes in Shenengo
Creek on a Friday afternoon and paddle
some fifteen miles northeast to Fox
Island Nature Preserve. There they would
set up camp in the dark and spend the
rest of the weekend hiking, cooking, and
sleeping outdoors. It was a real chance
to put all of our scout skills to the test,
and for Emile it had one very significant
added bonus: it was only open to boys in
high school. Regardless of my rank and
investment in the troop, I wasn't allowed
to go that first year.

When the weekend finally arrived,
my mother and I stood on the sloping bank
of the Shenengo, behind the V.F.W., as the
older boys and their fathers pushed off.
I couldn't help but feel a little dickless
as we watched the canoes disappear.
My mother must have sensed this would
happen because she purchased two tickets
for us to the opening night game of the
Buffalo Bisons, the AAA minor league

affiliate of the Pittsburgh Pirates who
played their games in Buffalo's crumbling
War Memorial Stadium. But twenty minutes
after the canoes turned out of sight, as
my mother and I were driving to the city
to catch the game, the rains came.

We waited in the concourse of the
stadium for two hours, only to learn
the game would be rescheduled for a
later date. All we had to do was bring
our ticket stubs back on the day of the
rescheduled game, and we'd be able to see
it for free. My mother offered to buy two
tickets to the game the next day, but I
said I'd rather not drive into the city
again. It was a good thing I did too,
because the rain didn't stop until Sunday
afternoon.

The clouds broke just as we headed
down to the V.F.W. to meet my brother and
father as they paddled back up the creek.
They arrived on time and made jokes about
the weather as they unpacked their gear
from the canoes. Emile was as happy as

I had ever seen him, but my father was
tired and uncharacteristically short
with the other boys.

Emile went to bed early that night.
I was in my room doing the homework I
had neglected all weekend when I heard
the edges of an argument rising from the
living room. I abandoned my books and
crept down the hall, lying on my stomach
to listen as my father spoke in a loud
whisper that betrayed his anger and
frustration.

"Well, I was wrong to think it.
Things have changed, Marty."

"Is it possible you're overreacting?"

"He brought guns to the camp-out.
Handguns."

"Isn't there some merit badge
related to shooting guns?" my mother
asked.

"Rifle shooting," my father said,
indignantly. "They shoot at targets in
that badge, Marty, not wildlife. The crazy
bastard had them shooting at squirrels
with handguns. We were in a goddamn

nature preserve."

"Frank, calm down."

"Do you want to tell me how calm
you would be if you woke up to gunshots
outside your tent? I've got to report
it, Marty. I've got to go to the council
with it. Gerehart is dangerous. In good
conscience I just can't let him be around
those boys."

"Frank, you do what you need to do,
but know this: Emile loves Bob Gerehart.
For whatever reason, he sees him as a role
model."

"Right, that is exactly the
problem," my father explained. "Do you
know the Scout Motto, Marty?"

"No."

"It's 'Be Prepared.'"

"Okay."

"Well, I woke this morning to Bob
Gerehart lecturing a handful of teenaged
boys about gun responsibility. Get this,
he told those boys--Emile was one of them-
that 'Be Prepared', in principle, meant
carrying a gun."

"What exactly did he say?"

"He said, 'Part of being prepared is knowing how to face down your enemy-- knowing how to handle yourself in a fight.' This is Boy Scouts we're talking about, Marty, not the Marine Corp."

"I thought teaching Emile how to handle himself in a fight was one of the reasons you signed him up."

"Not like this, Marty."

"Well, what were the other men doing while this was going on?"

"They're all N.R.A guys. You know that."

"What did Emile do?"

"He was the first to volunteer to shoot the thing."

"Emile fired a gun?" As she listened, my mother's tone evolved from discounting to comforting to questioning, and had now clearly crossed the line into anger.

"Not only did Emile fire it, but he killed a squirrel on his first shot. He's a natural born pistol-packer, according to Bob Gerehart." My father abandoned his whisper at the last syllable of Gerehart's name.

"Why are you guys talking about Mr. Gerehart?" Emile asked stepping over me into the living room. I had no way of knowing how long he had been standing behind me, how much he heard, but something in the way he looked down at me as he carelessly stepped over my head told me he knew what they were talking about. "Don't tell me you've got some problem with him, Dad."

My father's initial surprise at seeing Emile quickly turned to genuine anger. "Emile, go to bed. We'll talk about this in the morning."

"No!"

"Emile! That's enough!" my mother shouted, but my brother waved her off.

"What is your problem, Dad?"

"The man is sick, Emile. He's sick."

I could see the tension rise in Emile's posture. My father's words seemed to physically strike him.

Nothing Here is Real

"Why? 'Cause he's willing to fight back? 'Cause he doesn't let people walk all over him like you do?"

"Go to bed!" my father repeated. "We'll talk about this more tomorrow."

"You're just jealous is all!" Emile shouted back.

"Emile!" My mother stood up. Her tone stopped both of them short. "We're all tired now. We'll talk about this in the morning." Then, almost as an afterthought, she added, "All this shouting is going to wake up your brother."

"My brother," smiled Emile, "is listening in the hallway." I scurried to my room before my presence could be confirmed. Hours later, with the pillow over my head, I finally fell asleep, ignorant of the argument's resolution.

When I came home from school the next day, Emile wasn't there. I looked in his room and found it uncharacteristically clean and orderly, his merit badge sash draped across his pillow. He hadn't left a note of any kind. My mind began racing with possibilities of where he could be and a deep sense of fear filled my chest at the thought of my parents arriving home from work to find him gone. Somehow I felt I would be blamed, so although I knew he would resent my doing so, I decided to go looking for him.

I found him, not far off the trail we used as a shortcut through Worthingdale Woods. He held my father's hatchet in his right hand and a dead branch in his left. "Hey," he said casually, as if he had been expecting me. He chopped the hatchet into the trunk of the tree and without further explanation said, "Follow me."

I followed Emile deeper into the woods through a series of scattered trails. As the canopy of the still-budding trees began to thicken, the undergrowth thinned, and I was able to see a larger trail I had never been on before emerging. Emile was jogging now, and I hustled to keep up. He was a good twenty yards in front of me when he looked over his shoulder and said, "Watch yourself on the hill." He descended out of sight down the slope of a gully.

When I reached the top, I saw Emile stopped on its downward slope with his pants around his ankles, emptying the contents of his bladder. Sensing my presence he lifted a hand with a closed fist to stop me.

He shook himself off, pulled up his pants, ducked into a crouch, and waved me forward. When I was standing next to him, he swept his hand across the trail to indicate the thin wire strung between two shin-high stakes on either side of the path.

"You didn't see it, did you?" he asked.

"No. What's it for?"

"It's a trip-wire. It's not attached to any explosives or anything, but if anyone were to come running down this hill, it would likely cause them to trip and be thrown the few feet to the bottom of the gully." Then he stood and walked a few paces. "I figured once they fell, they would end up right about here." With the toe of his boot, he brushed aside a pile of leaves that were gathered where he stood. A cluster of thumb-thick green sticks, stripped of their bark, shaved to a point, and thrust into the ground so that the collective spearheads pointed upward toward the slope of the hill, revealed themselves.

"What're those for?" I asked.

Emile struck a professorial tone. "It's a tiger trap. The VC generally didn't have access to large collections of weapons, so they'd use whatever they could get their hands on to maim the GIs. You piss on them for insurance. That way, if the wounds they get from the spears are superficial, the infection that'll spring up from being stabbed by piss-covered sticks will still be enough to at least make them unable to fight for a long time."

"How do you know all this?" I asked him. He shrugged and thumbed his hand over his shoulder and said, "The hutch is up here."

I followed him up the opposite slope of the gully. At the top of the rise, I saw an extensive lean-to. Emile tossed the dead branch he had carried onto an open space in the structure's back wall and waved me inside. He had skillfully positioned a collection of limbs lengthwise at right angles so that they had the look of the triangularly stacked fences that still guard Civil War battlefields throughout the South.

"This place is awesome. When did you build it?"

"Today," he said. "I skipped school. We were planning on building it for a while." He stood back and looked at what he had created with a genuine sense of pride.

"You and who else?" I asked.

"Nobody. Just me."

"But you said 'we'."

"I built it myself," he said flatly. "Not bad, huh?"

I nodded silently. "But what's it all for?"

A broad smile crept across his face: "You." He could tell from my expression that I didn't fully understand, so he sat down on the worn floor of the shelter and told me his plans for the water war in Worthingdale Woods.

"Nothing crazy," he said, "just kind of a modified game of capture the flag. We'll do it this Saturday. That'll give us the week to gather our supplies. We'll use water balloons for grenades, super-soakers for missal launchers, and the standard squirt guns for the hand-to-hand stuff." I'm sure my face registered fear because he quickly added, "You won't get hurt unless you're stupid about it. "Besides," he shrugged, "we'll each have a home base. This hutch can be yours. I'll build mine by the sports field."

He went on to explain that, just

like capture the flag, the goal was to
get the other team's flag and bring it
safely back to your own home base without
getting tagged. But our water war had
to be different because there weren't
teams. If you got tagged, and therefore
captured, there was no way you could be
rescued--you had no teammates to set you
free. Instead, the way it would work is
if someone succeeded in getting the other
guy wet, the wet guy had to surrender
the weapons he was carrying to the enemy.
Once he handed over his ransom, he would
have five minutes to escape before his
enemy could try to track him down again.

"But what's the deal with the tiger
trap?"

"We just have to be careful, that's
all. We both know it's there."

"But why go to the trouble of
building it, and hiding it?"

"Simple," he smiled. "Fear. To put
that little question in the back of
both of our heads. That's why we lost
in Vietnam. We were afraid of what

might be there. Ho Chi Min, when asked
how he planned to defeat the U.S., said
something like, 'Even if you kill ten of
our men for every one we kill of yours,
even at those odds, we will win and you
will lose.'"

"That's crazy," I said.

"Yes, it's crazy, but it's also
brilliant. It rattled the U.S. soldiers.
They saw their enemies as crazy men who
would stop at nothing to win. It's like
Mr. Gerehart always says: all the evil
has been bleached out of the little, safe
world we live in. There's nothing to give
us an edge. That's why I built the trap."

"To give us something to be afraid
of?"

"Right. And to learn to face it."

"Do you have other traps?" I asked.

"Maybe," he said, smiling into the
shadows. "So how about it?" he asked. "Do
you want to play?"

Emile and I never spoke directly of
the events in the graveyard, but I knew
he knew I had watched, doing nothing to

stop it until it was too late to matter,
just as I knew he knew it was me who had
told his side of the story to Allen, who
in turn told Mary, prompting the fight in
the first place. In the days since, he had
barely acknowledged my existence, so for
him to suddenly include me in his plans
shocked me into suspicion.

But the more my brother spoke, the
more I realized the truth. He was lonely.
To my mind, it was bad enough I had twice
watched his social destruction without
doing anything to stop it. I couldn't
betray him again by refusing to fight.

"Okay," I said. "Let's do it."

Later that week, as Emile and I
sat doing our homework at the dining
room table, my father called me into the
kitchen. "Opening day is rescheduled
for this Saturday." He sat at the table
pointing to a small notice on the bottom
of the Sports page of The Buffalo News.

"What's that?" my mother called from
the other room.

My father explained, "Remember
how you and Grady got rained out of the
opening night of the Bisons?"

"Yes."

"Well, a scheduling quirk has
Pawtucket coming to town again this
weekend, and they're going to play the
make-up game as the top-half of a double
header, this Saturday. All you have to do
is bring your old tickets, and you'll get
in.

"That's great, Grady" my mother
smiled at me as she walked into the room.
"We'll get to catch the game."

I was thrilled with the thought of
going to the game because it meant the
water war was off. Sure, there was part of
me that had been pleased to be included
in Emile's plans, but the more I thought
about it, the more I couldn't shake the
reality of the tiger trap with its fatal
spikes buried below the leaves.

"Did you say it was on Saturday?"
Emile asked.

"Right, opening night has been

rescheduled for Saturday," my father read. "They're even going to do the fireworks after the second game, like they would have at the opener."

"Are you sure it's on Saturday, Dad?"

"Yes," my father said, tapping his finger on the small article in the paper. "Take a look for yourself." But Emile had already left the room without so much as glancing at the paper.

To this day, the game against Pawtucket remains the single most exciting baseball game I ever witnessed. Both pitchers carried no-hitters through the fifth. In the sixth, the Bisons broke it up with a slicing single to right. Shaken, the opposing pitcher gave up three consecutive towering shots: a long fly-out to center; a ground-rule double that bounced over the left field wall, scoring one; and a two-run homer smashed over the upper deck in right by sweet-swinging Harry Mo Brown, the Bisons' hulking, left-handed catcher. Pawtucket

broke up the Bisons' bid for the no-no
with their next ups, and the Bisons
didn't score again through the bottom
half of the eighth. Pawtucket battled
back to tie the game at 3-3 in the top of
the ninth. Their reliever struck out the
side in the bottom of the ninth, sending
the game into extra innings.

Halfway home, my mother was still
clamoring uncharacteristically in
the car about the deep solo-shot Brown
crushed to center in the bottom of the
twelfth to walk off with the Bisons' win.
"Too bad Emile and Dad didn't get to see
that, huh? I bet even Emile would have
found that exciting."

"Yeah, maybe," I said, but with
the mentioning of my brother's name,
the excitement of the game's stirring
conclusion was thrown to the outreaches
of my brain. For the rest of the ride home
my only thoughts were of Worthingdale
Woods.

It was an unseasonably hot day.

Nothing Here is Real

By the time I reached the woods, the sun
had been past its midpoint for a handful
of hours. Still, pools of noontime heat
lingered to breathless effect. I walked
down the trail, searching for Emile's
presence in the shadows.

Although the woods were open to
the public, the close proximity to school
seemed to scare off most of the other kids
in town, so when I heard broken voices
coming through the trees in the direction
of Emile's fort, my palms began to sweat.

I walked with a quickened pace as
the scattered saplings gave way to the
wider gully trail. The sun cut through
the canopy of maples and oaks in slanted
lines of light and shadow. The trail
reflected the movement of the trees,
darkening then awakening to the whims
of the turning leaves. As I approached
the hutch, the indistinguishable bramble
of sounds grew louder. When I crested the
lip of the gully, I saw at once why the
voices I heard seemed so foreign.

The brood of turkey vultures

gathered at the bottom of the hill did not squawk or call out sharply, but rather seemed to be whispering to each other in a language lost in time. With clucks and low, chesty rumbles they hovered over the body and picked at the pieces of red and exposed flesh with a symphony of ruffled wings and raised heads. They hardly knew I was there.

From where I stood, I could not see whose bones the birds were picking dry. As I ran down the slope, screaming the fears of my heart, the birds rose as one being from the ground and scattered to the upper branches of the shady trees, squawking fiercely in defense of their meal.

Standing in the belly of the gully, I saw the body of a small deer. The fawn's front forelock twisted in an unnatural angle was all the evidence I needed to know that the trip-wire had done its job.

The force of the animal's unnatural fall had thrust its body onto Emile's spears, but the creature's youth begot a

slight frame, and despite falling fully
onto the instruments of death, its weight
was not enough to push its body wholly
to the ground. In this way the flank of
the fawn lay suspended in air, two inches
in some spots, in others as high as four.
The feasting birds had torn the flesh
free from the wounds that now gaped with
cartilage and flecks of broken bone.

The head hung fully intact; its
nose, now muddy with its own blood, on
the ground as if to pick up the scent
of some unknown enemy. The fawn's eyes
were lashed and open. In the fractured
light, I saw my contorted face in their
glassy reflection; then, in their opaque,
lifeless mirrors, I saw I wasn't alone.

Emile stood at the top of the
gully. Stripped to his boxer shorts, his
body--a mass of sparse muscles, sinews,
and protruding bones--was streaked with
dirt and the blood of the fallen deer.
He looked down the slope to where I stood
next to the broken body. The birds fell
silent. Our eyes met in the darkness. I

knew him then as I never had before. At
last, my brother had found his enemy.

                              - G. Pickett
                    Apollo, NY - October 8, 2010

HAUNTINGS

1.

He was writing the question on the board as the students filed in that Friday: *What is your biggest regret?* After the bell rang, Ty asked, "You want us to tell you that?" Grady turned around to face the class.

"No," he replied. "I want you to take out a sheet of paper and write it down. What did you do? Why did you do it? What were you thinking at the time? How did it feel then? Why do you regret it now? Write it out." With that, Grady took out a sheet of paper, and bending over it, began to write. After a few minutes, he looked up. Everyone was writing except Seamus Clelland, who had laid his head down on his desk and pretended to snore loudly.

After writing half a page, Grady quietly scanned the room. Some of the students were done and sat looking back at him patiently.

"Two more minutes," Grady announced. Seamus Clelland pretended to jump awake. He wiped imaginary drool first off his face, then his desk, and sat smirking at Grady, waiting to play his hand.

As Grady started speaking, the students put their pens down and listened. "When I was thirteen years old,

Nothing Here is Real

I had a best friend. Chris Mendel. His dad was stationed at the Niagara Falls Air Force base, but his family lived in Apollo anyway, because the schools there were supposed to be better.

"They moved into the house that was kitty-corner from ours after the old guy who used to live there left. We hit it off right away. One day during the summer, Chris came to my house with a metal bucket and a net in his hands. He told me over the weekend he had been walking along Shenengo Creek and had seen tons of tadpoles swimming in the shallows by the entrance to the Water Street tunnel. You guys know where that is?" Some of the students nodded, but most sat still and silent.

"Anyway, it doesn't matter where it is. He wanted me to come with him and catch some tadpoles. He only wanted to catch the young ones, the ones who hadn't started growing legs or anything yet, the ones who were still basically fish. The idea was we would catch them and keep them as pets for a while, watch them turn from fish to frogs. Then, once they were frogs, we'd sell them to the little kids in the neighborhood. I was terrible at saving money and was always looking for ways to line my pockets with some change, so I went along with him, even though I was pretty sure no one would buy the frogs.

"Anyway, by the end of the morning, we had over

a hundred of the little guys in the bucket. Chris was much better at catching them than I was. He sort of gave me a hard time about it. Joking around and all, but still, he made a point of letting me know I hadn't caught as many as he had.

"As we walked up the street toward my house, Chris put the bucket down because the water was sloshing around and his arm was getting tired. He told me it was my turn to carry it. But you know what I did instead of picking it up?" He waited a moment to gauge their attention. "I kicked it over. Just with the side of my foot. Like nothing. I kicked it over. The water poured out all over the sidewalk and the tadpoles were carried with it. Some of them sloshed into the grass, but most of them just flopped there on the sidewalk. See, they were young. They hadn't developed their frog lungs yet. They might as well have been fish." Every kid in the room had his eyes on Grady.

"I remember Chris scurrying around the water stained sidewalk, trying to figure out a way to save them. All the water was out of the bucket. There were hundreds of them. There was nothing he could do. I'll never forget the look on his face. He said, 'Pickett, why'd you do that?' And I didn't know what to say, so I just picked up the bucket and walked home."

"You wrote that whole story down in like five

minutes?" Michelle asked.

"No, I just wrote the outline. I knew what I was going to tell you."

"You, like, just killed all those tadpoles for no reason?" Logan asked. Grady nodded. "That's, like, evil."

"I totally agree," Grady said. "I wish I had an excuse, like it was an accident or something, but I don't. To be honest, even today, I don't really know why I did it. But what I do know is that's the last time Chris and I ever hung out."

"He totally friend-dumped you because you were an evil frog killer," Seamus said, but no one acknowledged him.

"Truth be told, he was probably the best friend I ever had," Grady continued. "I'm pretty sure if I tried to talk to him about it, or if I had gone back to the creek and gathered some more tadpoles, that eventually things would have been okay between us. But I didn't do any of that, and so he just faded into the sea of other faces in the hall. Maybe a year later his family moved away." Grady waited a moment in the stillness of his classroom before continuing. "It's a sad story, no doubt, but the reason I'm telling it is this: I gave up a great friend all because I wasn't willing to say sorry. Looking back, it's like my whole life, I thought of myself as one type of guy, and in that instant, I became someone else." The class was silent.

"Listen, the reason I asked you to do this exercise, ladies and gentlemen, is I want you to think about Daisy's life from the inside-out. She knows that Tom is awful. She has a chance for a different life. Gatsby offers that to her, but she rejects it. Why does she stay with Tom?"

"For the money," Chaz offered.

"It's easier," Mindy said.

"Yes and yes. But I also think Daisy is pretty stubborn, isn't she?" Grady asked. "Going with Gatsby would be like admitting the life she's living is really pretty meaningless. The stakes are that high. So instead of acknowledging her mistake by taking action to change it she's got to cultivate this myth that her life with Tom is enough for her. So she stays and, Gatsby, the guy who tries to buy the world to win her heart, ends up dead at the bottom of a pool."

"But Gatsby's got some myth-issues too, though," said Mindy. "I mean, he's basically trying to undo the past. But you can't fix it, you know."

"Fair enough, but for today, let's just think about Daisy." He looked around the room to see if they were with him.

"The question is this: how do we get over the regrets of our lives? How do we move forward? Is it as simple as saying sorry? What if there is no way to undo the things we have done? Is it ever okay to just walk away?"

Again, the room was silent.

2.

Susan called two days later and after promising him that nothing was "really wrong," asked, as firmly as she could, that he join her for dinner at her place. There were some things she needed to tell him. Having not seen her since she left him to face Keith Clelland alone at The Well, and considering she called him at work to make the invitation, Grady was sufficiently curious and agreed to come over. He arrived on Susan's doorstep dressed in clean blue jeans, a white oxford shirt, and the tweed jacket he wore when he wanted to look sharp. He carried with him a bottle of red wine.

They drank a glass together and sat close on the couch, commenting on the weather and the joys of good food. Susan was wearing pearls and a clinging cotton dress with a low-cut neckline. Her lips were painted a dark shade of red.

When the small talk ran its course, Grady smiled and said, "So you've got me here, Susan. I'm dying to know what's up. I mean the last time I saw you, you were heading to the ladies' room at The Well. I hope you didn't fall in."

He was pleased to see she received his attempt at

humor as he offered it—a sign there were no hard feelings. "Yeah, Grady, that's what I wanted to talk to you about." But before she could continue the timer for the pot roast rang, and she excused herself to the kitchen to dish up their meal.

As she served their plates in the dining room, Grady set out napkins and poured each of them another glass of wine. Once their plates were full, Susan looked up at Grady over the steaming food. "I was early that night at The Well. I ordered us a pitcher and was just kind of sitting there when Keith Clelland pulled up a chair across from me."

"What?"

"Yeah, he pulled up a chair. It was pretty obvious he was drunk. Pretty dumb of him, if you think about it. I mean, I am one of the principal attorneys working on the case against his family business. Not exactly the person you want to go slurring your speech in front of at a local bar. But then again, he doesn't seem to get those kinds of nuances."

"He's an idiot," Grady said, shaking his head.

"He asked me if I was drinking alone, and when I told him I was meeting you there, he kind of went off."

"What do you mean?"

"It was tough to really figure out what he was

getting at, but the gist of it was he saw you and I as a perfect match—'arrogant assholes, made for each other,' I believe is how he put it."

"He said that?"

"He promised to buy a round for the bar once you arrived, in honor of us finally finding each other."

"What a jerk."

"I was going to tell you, but I didn't want to overreact. If you give guys like that the slightest reason to think you're afraid of them, then it's basically over, you know?"

"Totally."

"But, after you mentioned Briarly so sweetly... I didn't want to risk Clelland saying those things. I knew you didn't need that, Grady. I didn't want to hurt you any more than you've already been hurt. I mean, it seems like whatever happened is still pretty raw."

Grady could tell she wanted him to explain the missing details, but he remained silent.

"That's why I left. I figured with me gone, he wouldn't have any reason to make a scene."

"Well, that was kind of you, Susan."

She turned her head sideways toward the kitchen, so he couldn't see the tears she felt stinging her eyes. She got up for more wine.

When she returned, Grady said, "I see the For Sale sign is still up. The house looks great."

"Yeah, the market is awful, so you've got to do everything you can to bait the hook for potential buyers."

"Aw, don't tell me that," Grady said, tossing his napkin on his lap.

"Are you looking for a place? I thought you were going to be staying at your parents' this year."

"No, I can't do that anymore. Too many ghosts. I moved out. Actually, the night at the bar was my first night in my new place."

"Where's your new place then?" she asked plainly.

"Above the insurance office on Water Street. It's actually the apartment Ward Gregory grew up in."

"Oh... have you been haunted yet?" she said rubbing her hands together. Grady shook his head and chuckled. "That wasn't an answer, Mr. Pickett," she said.

"Something like that, I guess," he said without the hint of a smile.

"You're serious?" she asked. He nodded in reply.

"Tell you what," Susan offered. You go make yourself comfortable in the living room. I'll clean this up and bring out some dessert. Then let's see if you can scare me a bit."

At first he set out only to explain how he came to rent the Gregorys' place, but into his third glass of wine he found himself telling Susan about his family's relationship to the artist, and the role the Picketts played in the discovery of his death. She sat silently listening, only moving to put her empty cake plate on the ground and to draw her now shoeless feet sideways underneath her as Grady revealed his brother's accusation against Ward Gregory.

When he finished his story he looked at her plainly and said, "So now he's haunting me, I think."

"What do you mean?"

"I mean, the very first night I slept there I woke up in the middle of the night to this deafening sound of crows cawing outside of my window."

"And were there crows there?"

"Yeah, hundreds of them."

"Okay, now I'm scared," Susan said, attempting to kid away the seriousness of Grady's expression.

"Me too," Grady said flatly.

"So, let's just set aside the craziness of what you've told me for just a second and, for the sake of argument, imagine that what you saw was real and not the result of some weird mixture of stress and bad food–what do you think it means?"

"I don't really know," Grady admitted. "Maybe someone—Ward Gregory probably—just wants to make sure I'm paying attention."

"You're serious about all of this aren't you?"

"Yeah, I mean what other choice do I have? I saw what I saw, didn't I?"

Susan got up to take the dessert dishes out to the counter. She returned with their wine glasses full once again, dimming the lights as she came. "I really don't get it," she said, as she sat down next to him, handing him his glowing glass.

Grady took a long, thoughtful drink. "This is good stuff."

"Come on," she said. "You're starting to worry me."

"Worry you? Why?"

"Why? Oh, I don't know, Grady. First you tell me this crazy story about your brother being violated and your mother finding the body of the perpetrator hanging in his garage, and then you tell me you've chosen to move into the creep's apartment, and now you're being haunted. Really? And you're asking me why I'm concerned?"

Grady laughed and took another drink.

"Seriously," Susan added. "I'm worried about you."

"Susan, you don't need to be worried about me. I know exactly what I'm doing."

"What are you doing, then? Why are you living in that apartment, Grady?"

"This isn't some game," he said. "If that's what you're suggesting."

"No, I just... I guess it just seems like a pretty in-your-face move on your part. If I were your brother, I would wonder what you're trying to prove. Of all the places in Apollo, why live there?"

"That's a fair question," he said. "I guess the whole truth is, as I grew older I started seeing inconsistencies, not just in Emile's story, but in everything around me associated with my family."

"What do you mean?"

"Well, take my parents for example. They've always professed this great, abiding love for each other, high school sweethearts and all of that, but my father—he lives his life like some sort of passive ghost. It's like he doesn't even inhabit his own body anymore. He's just an extension of my mother's will. And she lets it happen. She's constantly on the verge of snapping at him or exploding into madness at the tiniest suggestion of a slight. And then there's Emile. For as long as I can remember, he's been fighting just to fight. It's like he actively seeks out ways to alienate people. After a while, it all sort of seemed put on to me. Like their lives were just some big act. I guess I felt like I had to figure out how it got to be that way for them, so that it wouldn't get to be that way for me too. Does that make any sense?"

"But what does this have to do with living in Ward Gregory's old apartment?"

Grady leaned forward. "I just feel like this is where I have to start. The only way to know the truth is to get a good look at it. Something tells me I'm supposed to live there. I just feel it. I know that sounds weird." Susan stared at him, transfixed by the earnestness of his reply.

"And what if next time it isn't just crows you hear outside your window? Aren't you worried about Emile's reaction when he finds out you're living there?"

"Emile is harmless. Either way," he said, "you've got nothing to worry about. I'm fine." But as Grady walked away from Susan's door an hour later, his eyes full of tears after kissing her goodnight, he wasn't so sure.

3.

Crosby Gibbons was pacing in the front of the room when Grady arrived late for lunch duty. The period was only seven minutes old, but Grady could see as he entered the room, the table of freshmen was already divided; each boy was sitting in a different corner of the cafeteria.

"You're here early," Grady laughed at the art teacher.

"Well, one of us should be."

"I see you've moved the table of thugs to their separate corners."

"Right. I got sick of talking to the little bastards."

"Where's Colin?"

"I told him he could eat his lunch in my classroom. The kid's a pretty good artist. He seemed grateful for the time alone."

"You sure he's okay in there? I mean, leaving a kid all alone in your room could get you in some hot water."

"This place is so full of shit," Crosby said. "It didn't used to be this way. Used to be if you were doing something in the best interest of the kid, you got the benefit of the doubt. Now everybody's all caught up in the bullshit. Safety, and all that. There's nothing safe about the world today, and no one knows that better than these kids."

Grady chuckled. "Shit, Gibby, I didn't know you cared."

"I don't," he said. "I'll be right back. I forgot my lunch."

Grady walked slowly around the room, pacing the rows of tables with his hands clasped behind his back. When he returned to the front of the room, Gibby was back with his lunch. "The kid's fine," he said.

"What kid?"

"Colin. I just went and checked on him. He's working on a painting."

"He didn't have the razor blades out?"

"Shit, the kid is depressed, but he's not that depressed."

"You know, speaking of depressed kids," Grady ventured, "I wanted to ask you about this Ward Gregory show. Everybody in Apollo is very hush, hush about the paintings."

"Of course they are," Gibby said. "Part of the deal is they want to build up the excitement about them."

"But you're an art guy. Do you know anything about how this woman got her hands on them?"

Gibby grinned. "Anita Kennedy can be a bitch, but she's damn good at what she does, and that's collect art. She, like everybody else, heard the rumors about the lost paintings. She's always wanted to open a gallery in Apollo—probably thought all the loaded snobs out there would make her rich. Anyway, she must have figured since Gregory lived in Apollo, getting those painting and showing them would be a hell of a way to open a gallery. Everybody loves a dead artist. It cracks me up."

Grady interjected, afraid if he let Crosby ramble he would lose him for good. "But where did she find the paintings? I mean people must have been looking for them for years. How did she get them?"

"The rumor downtown is after they found him dead, the police took the paintings and hid them in some barn on the outskirts of town, so all the media whores wouldn't go trying to capitalize on them. The guy had no family, and I guess he didn't leave a will, so they just stored them, hoping someone would figure out what to do with them. But the problem was that only a few of the cops on the force knew where they were. Of course, no one really believed that story because it just sounded too cheesy to be real, but then Anita Kennedy comes along, and she believes it. So what she does, she gets all dolled up and goes driving 100 miles per hour down Water Street in Apollo–

literally100 miles per hour. It's like three o'clock in the morning when she does it, so she has to take a couple of laps before she finally gets pulled over."

"Why would she want to get pulled over?"

"She wanted the paintings. I'm telling you she's as crazy as a shit-house rat." Gibby laughed. "Hey, start picking up your crap. The period ends in about ten minutes. I'm not your dad, and I'm not gonna pick it up for you," he shouted at the table in front of them.

"So how does getting pulled over... "

"I'll tell you, if you let me finish," the older man chided.

"Sorry, go ahead."

"Well, she knows damn well you get your license revoked if you're driving like that, so the cops impound her car and take her to the station. They book her for reckless endangerment. She's happy as a clam, though, because there she is, in this little black dress, all made up and everything; she knows her plan is working. She wanted to get arrested."

"What the hell for?"

"She wanted to talk to the chief, and she wanted him to believe that she owed him a favor. See, Anita Kennedy is not only gorgeous; she's also charming as hell. So after Chief Bassett gets the morning report, he goes in to see her 'cause all the guys on the overnight shift can't stop talking about the babe they've got locked up in the cell. At first he comes in all serious, but she somehow sweet talks him and ends up not only getting out of the clink, but also getting her car back."

"What? How did that happen?"

"It might have had something to do with the little arrangement she made to meet Bassett that night at The Well for drinks."

"She made a date with him?"

"That's right, and no guy in his right mind, even an arrogant prick like Bassett, isn't going to be grateful when a woman like Anita Kennedy asks him out. Anyway, after a few rounds, she starts grilling him about Ward Gregory. By this time, 'ole Bassett's all oiled up and full of himself. She plays the 'being chief, you must know everything that goes on in this town' card, too. But the truth is, Bassett doesn't know shit about art. He wouldn't be able to tell you the difference between an oil and a watercolor.

"Anita Kennedy sees through all his bluster, and she's about to cut him loose, when he admits to her he doesn't know where they are, but he could make a few calls and find out. He steps out to call Hadley, the old, retired chief who had been in charge of the Gregory investigation, and begs the guy to tell him where the paintings are.

Nothing Here is Real

Of course, Hadley thinks Bassett is crazy, but he tells him anyway. Bassett returns to the table and invites Ms. Kennedy to take a drive with him out into the hills of Apollo.

"He's too loaded to drive, so he gives her the keys to his Hummer, and they go bombing over the hills in search of the barn where the paintings are. Now I guess Bassett thinks he's a pretty smooth guy because he directs her on this long ride out into the country. After they've been driving for a while he tells her to pull over, and he starts getting hot and heavy with her. She plays along until he whips out his crank and tells her he wants to bone her right there on the side of the road."

"How could you possibly know all of these details?" Grady laughed.

"Will you let me finish? You asked, didn't you?"

"So, she starts back fooling around with him, like she's into it, but right when he's all excited, she tells him she wants to see the paintings before she gives it up. He's so scared he's gonna get blue balls he agrees and takes her to this barn out in the middle of nowhere. So they go and after they paw around for a while they find the paintings buried underneath a whole shit-load of stuff the cops have confiscated over the years. Whoever put them there must have known a thing or two about art, cause they were crated up in a separate room within the barn, all nice and dry.

"Anyway, Bassett's thinking that he's about to get some action, but Kennedy's not giving it up. She tells him she doesn't want to do it 'in the presence of the paintings,' that she wants to go back to his place.

"Bassett is divorced and shares custody of his daughter with his wife. But the thing is, the bastard is so wasted and such a shitty father anyway, he can't remember whether or not this is the weekend his daughter is home. When they get to the house, he tells Anita he's got to run inside first to make sure the coast is clear. When he's inside, she drives off with his vehicle. He comes out, and she's gone."

"Where'd she go?"

"You're believing it now, aren't you?"

"No, I'm just waiting for you to screw up the story, so I can call you on it."

"Screw you, then. I don't have to tell you anything."

"Gibby, come on. The bell's gonna ring in a minute or so."

"Well, maybe you'll have to wait until tomorrow then."

"Come on, for God's sake."

Gibby was beside himself for a minute, then he

continued. "She drives back to the barn. The guy who owns the place, some guy about your age named Miller, sees Bassett's Hummer and doesn't think anything of it. She goes into the barn and gets the paintings, and takes them back to her gallery downtown. Then she drives back to The Well, drops off the Hummer, leaves the keys on the front seat, drives her own car home, and goes to sleep.

"Bassett calls her the next day mad as hell, threatening to arrest her on charges of prostitution, all kinds of shit, until she reveals that she was wired–she's got the whole evening on tape. She tells him she'll keep the tape to herself if he'll let her keep the paintings."

"That is a great story, but total bullshit."

"That's how she got 'em."

"No way anyone is that crazy."

"I'm telling you she is. That's Anita Kennedy. She's one crazy bitch." The bell rang, but the men remained talking.

"You still haven't answered how you came to know all of that. I mean all those details—those kinds of things don't just get passed along the rumor mill. Somebody would have said something to the papers by now."

"Oh, the rumors are out there, but I didn't hear about it that way."

"How'd you hear about it, then?"

"Anita told me herself," Gibby grinned. "I told her I'd donate one of my oils to her gallery if she'd tell me how she got a hold of Gregory's work. That's how I know she's not lying."

"Just because she told you all that stuff doesn't mean it's true."

"Anita Kennedy may be crazy, but that lady loves art."

"Yeah, Gibby, she may love art, but ladies sometimes lie."

"Maybe," Gibby said, as he turned to leave, "but tape recordings don't."

4.

For the first time in months, Grady went for a run when he got home from school that afternoon. A steady rain fell and brought with it the growing chill of an autumn evening. When he returned to the apartment he shed his clothes and stood under the shower letting the heat of the water soak into his skin. After he was dressed again, he went to the window and pulled open the sash. The rain was still falling. The large pine stood silent and foreboding before him. He had no idea what time it was.

A quick knock came on his door. He ignored it, sure it was in his head, but as he moved across the room to the kitchen to get some food, he heard it again.

He walked to the door and saw in the light that shone beneath its frame a pair of dome-like shadows cast by the feet of his visitor. "Who's there?" he asked, but only a knock came in reply. "Shit," he said under his breath, as he pushed the door open.

Susan stood with her wet hair held in one hand and her shoes in the other. Her shirt was soaked and clinging to her body. The water, dripping off the ends of her running shorts, left pools on the floor in front of Grady's door..

"I ran from home," she said, still clearly winded. "I needed some air. Plus, I saw you running. I figured I'd try to catch up to you, but you were too fast. Anyway, I took my shoes off when I got inside the door downstairs. Everything is soaked. I didn't want to squeak all the way up to your door." She shrugged and smiled.

"Why don't you come in?" he said. "I'll get you a towel, and some coffee." She smiled broadly and cast her eyes to the ground. He held the door for her. "I didn't know you're a runner."

"Oh, I'm not really," she said, as she walked inside. "I just go out sometimes when I'm feeling motivated."

"Like when it's pouring rain?"

"Yeah. It seemed like a good day, you know?"

"The bathroom is straight down the hall, the last door on the right. There should be a dry towel hanging on the rack in there."

"Okay, thanks," she said. "Can I leave my shoes here?"

"Yeah, that's fine." She walked past him down the hall, her wet clothes swishing against her goose-bumped skin. "I'll put the water on," he said.

When she closed the bathroom door, he walked into the kitchen and filled a pot with water. Then he turned on the stove. She came out of the bathroom with the towel wrapped around her hair, her clothes still washed through with rain.

"All dry," she laughed, raising her arms slightly.

"Listen, I've got a little built-in washer and drier off the bedroom. Why don't I loan you a pair of dry shorts and a shirt? That way you can dry your stuff while we talk in the kitchen."

"Yeah, okay," she shrugged. She followed him to the bedroom and watched as he pulled out some clothes from a trunk against the wall. He handed them to her and walked out of the room.

The pot on the stove was whistling when Susan padded barefoot into the kitchen wearing one of his old gray T-shirts and a pair of cotton, drawstring shorts bunched up at the waist with the string cinched tightly in a double knot. She did a graceful twirl as she walked into the room. "I bet you never thought you'd see me in your clothes, did you?" she laughed.

"There have been a lot of things happening lately I never thought I'd live to see," he said.

He fixed two cups, handing hers to her first, and then joined her at the table, cupping his steaming mug in his hands.

"So, Susan," he asked, "what's the real story?"

"What do you mean?"

"I mean why did you run to my apartment in the rain?"

"What's that supposed to mean? You don't believe I'm a runner?"

"Uh, no."

"Screw you, then."

"Seriously, what's the story?"

She laughed through the steam rising from the cup as she put it to her lips. "Well, to be honest, I haven't stopped thinking about your crow story. And with the gallery due to open this weekend, I figured I'd stop by and get a look at the place for myself."

"And you weren't worried about the fact that I might take you for a stalker?"

"Well. No. I guess I hadn't really thought about that."

"Hmm."

"I mean," she put her cup down. "Aren't we sort of beyond that now?" Grady said nothing in reply.

Susan pushed her cup into the middle of the table and leaned forward so that her wet hair tumbled from behind her ear and framed her glowing face. "I guess, your story isn't the only thing I haven't been able to stop thinking about."

Grady shifted in his chair, but didn't look away from her steady gaze. "Susan. The other night was nice. It's just . . ."

"Look, I know there's more to the story here, Grady. I'm not stupid."

"That's right."

"And, I don't know, I sort of feel like I'm entitled to know what I'm getting into."

"Getting into?"

"Maybe I'm way off here," she said, pushing her chair back in exasperation.

"No, wait." He reached across the table and grabbed her hand. "It's not that. It's just there's a lot going on. A lot I didn't expect."

"Well, you can't be prepared for everything," she said, sitting back in the chair and then leaning forward. "Sometimes we go looking for one thing and find something else."

"Yeah, I guess things happen the way they're supposed to happen, right?"

"Oh, you're one of those, *everything happens for a reason* guys?"

"Yeah, I guess. Why?"

"Grady, can I tell you a story?"

"Yeah," he said, sitting back in his seat. "I'm an

English teacher. I love stories."

She brushed imaginary crumbs off the table and began. "This one time my family and I were on vacation at the ocean. One night we ended up lying out all together by the water looking up at the stars. I mean, the sky just opened up before us. It was like we could see every star that ever was.

"We're lying there all quiet, when, all of a sudden, my dad points to the sky and says because stars are so far away, their light has to travel to our eyes over the course of hundreds of lifetimes, so the light we see now could in fact have been born of stars no longer burning."

"That's right," said Grady.

"Then he starts pointing out the constellations— Orion and all of that—telling us that they're what real faith in God is all about. Because for centuries men navigated their way across the world with nothing more than faith in the unchanging nature of the stars. He said it's almost like God put them there for that reason. To see if people would trust in his larger plan. Then my dad tells us that thinking of the stars this way should make us feel powerful." Grady was silent.

Susan shifted in her seat. She was holding the side of her face with an open right hand, her fingers pushed in slightly against her strong cheekbones. "I didn't say anything at the time," she continued. "Maybe I didn't know how to, or maybe I just didn't want to hurt my dad's feelings, but to me, looking at the stars that way—the constellations and all the history and science behind them—it just ruined it."

"Ruined it?" Grady asked. "How?"

"I just can't see how it could make him feel powerful. Measuring the distance and speed of the light, trying to find the Big Dipper, all of that just takes away the mystery and wonder of the sky and in its place slaps a science lesson." She took a drink of her coffee. "For a long time the beauty of the sky was ruined for me. It's like I couldn't see it with my own eyes anymore, you know? I mean, it just looked like someone else's imagination. Some things aren't meant to be explained." The last of her words were swallowed by the stillness between them. Susan continued, "See, things happen like what happened to your family—worse things even—and people all over the world find comfort in saying, 'Everything happens for a reason,' or 'All of this is part of God's plan.' Nobody wants to admit it's just random. So they all say, 'It's all part of God's plan.' But if that's the case then our lives are nothing more than Him coloring in the pictures in His cosmic coloring book. Some things just happen, Grady. It's up to us to act on them. If we admit that, then our lives are at least our own."

"But what's the purpose of our lives then, Susan, if everything is bouncing around without a string—totally left to chance?" His voice was strained with a tension she hadn't heard before.

"I dunno," she said. "But that's the beauty of it. We get to make it meaningful in our own way."

She looked at him across the table, but as she went to speak, he interjected. "You know, Briarly used to say something to me that I'll never forget. She used to say, 'The smallness of our lives confirms the infinite love of God.'"

"I don't understand," Susan said, her voice shallow now. "What does that mean, even? What does that have to do with what I'm talking about?"

"It means that you and I, Ward Gregory, Keith Clelland, all of us, even the most flawed, are blessed with the mixed-up fullness of life. We're alive. If you look at the universe scientifically, there's no logical explanation for why humans have survived as long as we have. All the exterior forces seem inclined toward extinction. But here we are, living out the spans of our tiny, seemingly meaningless, lives. And that made her feel holy."

"Just because we're alive?"

"Yeah, because we're alive and, by all scientific accounts, we shouldn't be. So, it's either God's will or the result of some collective cosmic accident with a million different coincidences lined up just so to create this one specific outcome. I guess she thought if we're brave enough to believe in God at all, then we've got to believe he wants us living. If you accept that, then it's not too much of a stretch to think we're here for a reason. His reasons. That's how we know our lives have purpose; he loves us enough to keep us alive."

"Okay, then how does she explain the Holocaust or 9/11 or even all the other, everyday people whose lives end before their time? Why did those things have to happen?"

"You know, that was the last thing she asked me before I left," Grady said. "'Why did this have to happen?'" He drank the rest of his coffee and set the cup back down on the table. He sighed and rubbed his hand across his forehead. "Our baby has been dead for more than six months now, Susan, and I still haven't figured out the answer to that one."

Susan looked down at her hands. "Oh. I didn't know. I mean, how did it happen?"

"It just did. We went in for our five-month appointment and the doctor told us they couldn't find a heartbeat. They didn't know why."

"My God."

"Later they told us it was a genetic abnormality. They didn't catch it in the screening process. There was nothing they could have done, anyway." He was looking past her into the open space of the apartment. "It was a little girl, the baby. We didn't find that out until after."

"Grady, I'm so sorry, I didn't know. That's awful."

"It's worse," he said, shaking his head. See the thing was, after we found out, we had to decide. Either Briarly had to go in to the hospital, be induced and go through the delivery knowing the baby was dead, or we had to go to a clinic."

"A clinic?"

"Yeah. The doctor we chose was affiliated with a Catholic hospital. And apparently they don't do the procedure, whatever it's called, that takes a five-month-old baby out of its mother after its dead. You have to go to an abortion clinic for that."

"What did you do?"

"I talked her out of delivering. I didn't want her to have to go through the pain. I thought maybe after that, she'd never want to have children. I thought it would be worse for her, but I was wrong."

"What do you mean? Did something happen?"

"When we pulled into the driveway of the clinic, we saw this group of protesters across the street holding signs. A police car was parked by the curb. There was a guard at the door to the clinic. We were too wrapped up in things to think much about it, though."

He was talking more to himself then to Susan. "The waiting room was set up in the shape of a U. There was this high counter in front of the reception desk with a thick sheet of bullet-proof glass in front of it. When we sat down, Briarly leaned her head against my shoulder. I kept saying things like, 'You're going to be all right,' but when that didn't work I said, 'Try to stop crying now. They need you to stop.' After a while she stopped and just sat there silently breathing against my arm.

"There was a woman sitting by herself in the last seat of the U, closest to the door into the clinic. Her hair was cut short. She was dressed for work. On her lap was an unopened magazine; her fingers drummed against the cover. I couldn't tell if the drumming meant she was waiting her turn, or if it was because she was anxious about her friend or sister who had already gone back. Later I decided it was the second one. She had to be waiting for someone else. No one wears heels to get an abortion.

"I just kept thinking, *This is an abortion clinic. These people are all here for abortions. We should have gone to the hospital.*

"Grady, don't do this to yourself."

Ignoring her, he went on. "In the opposite corner of the room, there was a small group of people, two women and one man. They were all about my age, maybe a few years younger. One of the women was large, her thighs spreading out onto the chairs on either side of her. The other woman was slim—tastefully made up. Her long hair was pulled back in a high bun, and her gold hoop earrings stood out against her thin neck. Neither of the women was noticeably pregnant. The guy was fat and, even though it was cold, he wore an oversized white T-shirt and a pair of plaid, knee length shorts. He was wearing one of those half-mesh baseball hats. I couldn't tell what team. And he wore these clouded glasses, but even from where I sat I could see his eyes. The three of them were chatting casually, even laughing from time to time. And that's when I started to really feel like getting sick. I mean, why would you be laughing?"

Susan raised her eyebrows, but said nothing in response. Grady continued as if she wasn't there. "The only other people in the waiting room were a pair of women, and looking at them, I was sure they were mother and daughter. Neither spoke. The daughter was probably in her twenties. She sat with her back slightly turned away from the mother. Her legs were crossed, and her foot was twitching in rhythm. She was chewing gum. The mother sat with her hands in her lap. She was wearing a beaded vest and a high-collared oxford shirt. Her hair was gray at the temples and stylishly bobbed. The creases on her slacks were impeccable. What I'm saying is, she looked very put together sitting there next to her daughter. She probably wanted grandchildren. Maybe she saw them as a chance to make up for the mistakes she made with her daughter. Who knows? But she was certainly sad, and her sadness made me look away. That's when I noticed the nurse walking toward us with a pile of papers in her hand.

"She told us I could go back with Briarly for a while, so she didn't have to wait in the room alone, but when it was time for the procedure, I had to leave."

"How was she when you left?"

"I don't know. I mean, I tried to prepare myself for what I'd see in there. But the lights were off, and there was one of those tables with stirrups on it to put your feet in."

"God," Susan whispered.

Grady continued in a hushed voice, "I'm pretty sure that's just the room they do the initial exam in, but still, the thought of her on a table, with her legs up like that, I don't know, it choked me up. I mean, she looked so scared. And after the nurse who took us back left the room, she kept asking me the same thing over and over again. And I didn't know what to say."

"What did she ask?"

"She wanted to know where they took the body.

'What's going to happen to the body once it's out of me? Will they bury it?' That's what she kept asking me.

    "After I got back to the waiting room, it was the weirdest thing. It was like I felt this swelling inside my head, and the lights of the room literally broke before my eyes. I mean, I was aware of the young girl sitting next to me, the voices from the others in the room, the shaking foot of the daughter next to the mother in the beaded vest, the magazines that sat on the tables next to the chairs, the bullet-proof glass in front of the receptionist, but it's like I couldn't make the scene work. I knew I was going to be sick, so I stood quickly and moved toward the door, but the guard stepped in my way.

    "He said something like, 'What's the rush, buddy?' and I told him to get the fuck out of my way. The next thing I remember is sitting in a different chair with a garbage can in front of me full of vomit. That's when I went to the front desk and asked them about the remains."

    "Oh no. Grady, what did they say?"

    "They tried to blow me off, to be honest. The nurse wouldn't look me in the eye. I suspect the truth is whatever horrible thing they do to get the body out, destroys it beyond recognition. But they didn't say that. I can't be sure exactly what they said. All I remember is the term 'medical waste,' and the nurse's firm hand leading me back to my seat in the waiting room. And that's where I sat until they walked Briarly out."

"How was she?"

"It was a miserable day. I mean the weather. That's the first thing I noticed when we got into the parking lot. There was sleet falling against the windshield. Then somebody shouted 'You've just killed your baby, you selfish bitch!'"

"What?" Susan asked, her eyes glassy with tears. Grady still wouldn't look at her.

"The protestors," he said. "'Baby killers don't go to Heaven.' 'Did they let you watch it die?' All that shit."

"What did you do?"

"Well, Briarly was half out-of-it because of whatever drugs they gave her, but still she was grabbing my coat and screaming at me to make them stop. All I wanted to do was get her in the car and get out of there, but I couldn't find my fucking keys. So I let go of Briarly to better search for them, and she just collapsed."

"Was she okay?"

Grady shook his head. "When I got the door open I gathered her into my arms. God, she was like dead weight. But as I went to release her, she grabbed my face like a wild animal. 'You've got to tell them, Grady,' she said. 'Tell them it wasn't my fault.' But I just closed the door..."

His voice was gone, and for a long time they sat there in silence, Susan rubbing his hands and Grady looking into the darkness of the other room, blinking away the tears that streaked his face.

Susan was the first to speak. "When did all this happen?" But Grady continued as if he hadn't heard the question.

"Briarly wouldn't get out of bed for three days. She hadn't told her parents she was pregnant. After we got back to our apartment, she asked me to call her mother, but I knew better. When she was finally able to talk about it, she thanked me for that. A couple of weeks later, it almost seemed like everything was going to be all right. Like we would be able to pick up where we left off."

"Where you left off?"

"Yeah, before we found out she was pregnant, I had been saving for a ring." Susan said nothing in response. That's when he finally looked at her.

"But I just couldn't do it, Susan. I just couldn't move on."

"I can't imagine what it must have been like," she said.

"We even went to see somebody. A grief counselor," Grady brushed the memory of it away with his hand. "He told me the reason I was struggling so much was that I didn't have closure. He told us to gather some of the things we had purchased for the baby and to burn them. That way we'd have ashes to bury. Can you believe that?"

"It's almost ghoulish."

"I know, but Briarly was desperate."

"Oh my God."

"We went camping, and did it in the fire there. The next morning Briarly scooped up the ashes into this metal box she brought with her. A few days later she gave me my half. That's when I knew I had to leave."

"What do you mean?" Susan asked.

"The next night we were back in our apartment. I couldn't sleep. I was just walking around, trying not to wake her. Eventually I came to this window in the back of the place that looked over the field behind the dorm. I twisted open the blinds and sort of cupped my hands against the window. I guess I wanted to look at the stars. I don't really know how to explain this."

"You don't have to, Grady."

"Suddenly I just felt this overwhelming feeling. I mean, I all at once felt the crushing smallness of the tragedies of my life. I mean how many men before me had looked at the stars? How many sought to resurrect the dead? How small is the glow given off by each human life? I moved out a week later."

"That poor thing."

"The truth is Susan, I couldn't stand the pain of being around her. Isn't that shameful?"

"You're only human, Grady."

"Yeah," he said rubbing the back of his hand across his eyes. "But sometimes even that isn't enough."

He got up from the table and walked into the living room. After a moment Susan followed behind him. She saw him standing at the back window looking out at the parking lot. Grady could feel her eyes on him, but he refused to turn until he'd blinked the tears away from his eyes.

"I guess my clothes are done," she said, at the sound that pierced the air between them. He turned around slowly and saw she had gone into the bedroom and was pulling them out of the drier.

She turned away from where he stood and pulled his gray shirt over her head. Her naked back shone out of the bedroom's shadowy darkness as Grady gazed at her through the glare of the hallway's light. She tugged on her sports bra, her back still to him. He watched as the material of her own shirt settled over the small of her back. Grady felt a stirring in his chest and turned away from it to look again into the darkness of the window, but the thought of her dimly lit form pulled his eyes back. She must have lost her balance for she stood, her shorts around her ankles, with her hand placed firmly on the wall beside her. Grady's eyes lingered on her hand, spread wide against the whiteness of the wall. Then she stood erect as he beheld her in the final motion of sheathing her legs in her shorts. First, they were just past her slightly bent knees, then she pulled them up quickly to her waist. For a moment she stood looking away and fully dressed. Then she turned to return to the place where he watched her. He spun quickly back toward the window, his face red with shame.

"I think I better go," she said, when she came back in the room. Grady said nothing. When he heard the door open, he turned to her.

"Susan, wait." She froze with her hand on the door. Slowly he walked up behind her. For a moment he let the warmth of his breath bathe her unmoving neck. Then she turned to face him. Her chest rose and fell with the pace of her breathing. Grady reached forward and took her wrist in his hand. She released her grip without question. "Just wait," he said again, softly. Then he pulled the door shut behind her.

5.

The sun was setting behind him as he made his way over the hills back toward school. He decided to take the seldom driven, tree-lined paths that traced the way from Apollo to the studio apartment he'd taken on the edge of campus, some three hours away from his boyhood home. The day was well into its second half, yet it was still unseasonably warm. Grady drove fast with the windows down.

He saw the car in the shadows on the side of the road, the hazard lights flashing, a figure in a skirt bent over next to the vehicle in the act of changing a tire. Her hair was long and fell over her shoulders. In the moment Grady passed she reached up with a hand and curled a stray, auburn strand behind her ear. He drove for another mile before he pulled the car around and headed back to see if he could help.

She was wearing flip-flops, a white skirt which hung just past her knees, and a sage cardigan sweater over a snug fitting tank top the shade of pale sunset. Her necklace hung in her face, and her cheeks were flush with the effort of loosening the lug nuts of the flattened tire. As Grady got out of the car, he heard her give a little grunt as she planted her feet at an angle and threw her body weight against the tension of the lug wrench she held with both hands against her chest.

"Do you have some help coming?" Grady asked.

On her knees now, she looked up at him through her hair. "Oh, hey," she said. Then, as if it were an afterthought, she added, "Nope, I got it." Grady put his hands in his pockets and walked across the road.

"You're not supposed to have the car up on the jack when you're loosening them," Grady said. "That's why the tire is moving. You don't have any leverage."

"Where were you an hour ago when I started all of this?" she asked, letting the lug wrench drop and getting to her feet, looking at Grady for the first time. With the edge of her fingers, she pushed her hair fully behind her ears to reveal hazel eyes, shaded from the sun with her grease-splattered left hand. "I'm a mess," she said, looking down at the streaks of dirt that ran the length of her skirt.

Grady nodded. "The thing to do is to get it down on the ground again. Then the lug nuts should come off pretty easily. If they're on really good, you can stand on the wrench, and they usually will loosen up. I can do it for you, if you want." He reached down and picked up the lug wrench.

She shook her head, "No. Now that I know what to do, I might as well finish the job." She took her hand down from her eyes and rubbed it against the side of the car, in an attempt to get the grease off. "I'm supposed to be at dinner in a half an hour."

Looking behind the car Grady saw that she'd gotten the spare out of the trunk. "Half an hour is plenty of time to get the flat off and the spare on. You'll be on the road in a few minutes. Is your dinner in town here?" Grady asked.

"No, that's the thing," she said, reaching for the lug wrench in his hand. " It's in Saratoga. My sister goes to school out there. It's some big awards dinner. I'm meeting my whole family there."

"That's a ways away," Grady said. He held the lug wrench by one end, and she held the other end in her right hand. Her left hand reached up again to shade her eyes.

"Yeah, no way I'm making it now," she smiled. "Once I get this changed, I think I'll head back to school and call them to let them know I'll be late. My sister'll hate me for it, but what can you do?"

"Where's school?" Grady asked.

"Clinton," she said.

"Don't you have a phone? You could have called someone."

"I guess I left it in my dorm," she shrugged, and when she did, Grady noticed for the first time she was beautiful.

"My phone's sitting in the passenger seat over there,"

he said, tilting his head backwards in the direction of his car. *Why don't you go sit in my car and call them. I'll change the tire."*

"No, really, I'm sure you've got some place to go. It's sweet of you to offer," she said, looking down at the lug wrench they held between them, "but I can do it. I just forgot about loosening them first is all."

Grady let go of the wrench. The weight of the tool in her hand alone made it swing down next to her side. Grady continued, "I don't really have anywhere to go. I'm just heading back to school myself. I'd like to do it for you. Then you can get on the road that much faster." She leaned to the right to get a look at his car.

"I'm not a serial killer or anything, if that's what you're worried about. I'm just heading back to school too."

"Well, that's good," she laughed. "My dad always told me to avoid getting into cars with serial killers."

"Good advice," Grady said, "but isn't one thing that makes a successful serial killer his ability to hide the fact that he is one?"

"Exactly my point" she said. "You could have a body in the trunk for all I know."

"No body in the trunk, I promise. Just a bag of laundry I'm taking back to school."

They both laughed. The sun cast their shadows

against the roadway as a semi-truck blew past them.

"Besides," Grady said. "I wouldn't be in the car with you, I'd be over here, changing your tire."

"With a tire iron in your hand," she smirked.

"It's a lug wrench," Grady corrected her, and if I were going to beat you to a pulp with it, don't you think I would have done so by now?"

"I don't know. Maybe you're one of those gentlemanly-type serial killers who likes to lure your unsuspecting prey to their death with chivalry."

"You've thought of everything," Grady said, raising his hands in defeat. "Can I at least wait on the other side of the road, until I'm sure you'll be all set?"

"You're a real knight in shining armor type, aren't you?"

"No, it's just that my dad always told me never to leave a beautiful woman on the side of the road to change a tire by herself without doing your damnedest to help her."

"I don't believe your father ever said that to you." She brushed her flushed cheeks with the back of one of her hands.

"Maybe not," Grady said. "But how about it? The phone's on the passenger seat." He reached again for the lug wrench. "The door should be open."

She let go of the wrench and reached in through the driver's side window of the jacked-up car to grab her bag *before crossing the street. She laughed over her shoulder at him as she opened his car door.*

It took him ten minutes to lower the car, loosen the lug nuts, jack up the car again, and get the tire on. He was in the process of lowering it back down when he noticed her standing next to him.

"Did you get a hold of her?" Grady asked.

"Yeah, my mom thinks I'll be able to make it for dessert if I hustle. I guess the dinner's kind of a drawn out thing."

"Well," Grady said, walking to the back of the car and leaning into it to return the jack and lug wrench to the trunk. "I put the flat in here. You should be fine to ride on the donut until you get to Saratoga, but I'd change it there before you head back to school." Grady wiped the sweat off his brow with the edge of his shirt.

"Thanks," she said, extending her hand.

Grady wiped his hand on his shorts and took her hand in his, shaking it with false formality. Then he tipped an imaginary hat, and striking up a sugary-sweet southern accent, he said, "The pleasure's all mine, pretty lady." She smiled at his foolishness, opened her door, and slid into the seat. He stood next to the car as she looked out the window at him.

"Seriously, thanks."

"Wait a minute," Grady said, taking a step toward her as she turned on the ignition. "Don't I at least get a name?"

Mimicking his southern accent, she batted her eyes and said, "My Daddy told me not to give my name to strangers—especially tall, dark, and handsome ones who insist on helping me along my way."

"This father of yours is full of insights."

"You don't know the half of it."

"I'm Grady Pickett," he said, extending his hand to her once again. "Now we're not strangers."

"I know who you are Grady," she said, ignoring his greasy hand. "But I have to go now." And with that, she put the car in drive and turned onto the road.

It wasn't until her car was out of sight that he crossed to his vehicle shaking his head and cursing himself for not insisting on her number. As he climbed into the car he saw his phone on the seat. His wallet sat open next to it, his driver's license slightly askew in its regular space. Then he turned the car on and glanced in the rearview mirror to check if it was safe to turn around and head back to school. As he did he saw what she had done.

"Briarly Slooth, Hamilton College," it said in eyeliner on the mirror. "Find me."

Nothing Here is Real

Grady woke from his dream cloaked in the gray morning's light. Just a dream, he reminded himself, shaking the image of Briarly from behind his eyes. He made his way into the bathroom to let cold water run over his face and naked body. When he finished he walked out into the apartment wearing the shirt and cotton drawstring shorts Susan had borrowed the night before. He found his breakfast on the table.

Susan was busy in the room where she had spent the night, pulling the sheets back up over the mattress and running her hand down the smooth, tight surface to erase any wrinkles that remained. She turned to look at him. The window was open behind her. The damp, cool air of the October morning rushed in through the silent branches of the pines.

6.

When school was over the next day Grady sat alone in his classroom, letting his mind return to the events of the previous evening. Wondering, as he did, if he would ever be able to return to who he was before.

On the threshold of the apartment, he had pulled Susan close enough to feel the firmness of her breast pressed tightly against his body. Neither of them spoke, but as they stared at each other unwaveringly, their mutual silence shook with the awe they felt in the face of the closed door. At last she bent her head forward, resting it against his chest. Before she could look up again, Grady had kissed her softly where the part of her hair split open onto the expanse of her forehead. Her hands wrapped around him. Then she slowly moved them down his back to his waist, stopping at the front pockets of his pants where her fingers curled inward, gently pulling him toward her.

"Go to the bedroom," he whispered. She looked up knowingly. In her eyes he saw what all men desire in the gaze of a lover, but he also saw fear. He was sure it was her fear that had broken him loose of the spell.

Nothing Here is Real

He had walked behind her, a hand on her back. She did not look at him as she made her way toward the bedroom, the middle finger of her left hand slung loosely through a belt loop of his jeans. When they got to the door she turned to face him, her eyes full of the mysteries of life that once solved, lose the desperate magic that brings them into the world. She placed her palms on his chest and rose on her toes, with anxious lips, to meet him.

"Shhh," he said instead. She stepped away into the darkness of the room. He remembered how the dim light had cast shadows across her face—how as she stood trembling before him, his whole body ached to reach for her–but something compelled him to turn away. As she tilted her head and crossed her arms, reaching down to the corners of her shirt to make herself bare before him, he simply said, "Susan, wait."

Her eyes, somehow full of the room's sparse light, flashed down, but then rose quickly to meet his. She stood small and shadowed by the frame of his bedroom door. "Will you come to me?" she whispered.

He took a step back and cleared his throat. "The light's still on in the other room," he said with a thick voice. Then he turned away and walked toward the kitchen where they had sat together talking of the stars.

Grady didn't know what Susan felt in those long

moments after he had shut off the light, just as he didn't know her touch upon his body, though he had longed for the comfort of it with all his being. He didn't turn back to her. Instead, he had walked to the back window of the apartment and stood looking out into the night. After a time, he pressed his hand gently against the thin glass. The coldness of the air licked the tips of his fingers. He stood half-dazed, as if willed by a force beyond his being. Somehow he knew she wouldn't come for him as long as he looked out into the night. When at last his legs could stand no more, he walked to the couch and let his dreams take him. He hadn't turned back.

Though they ate breakfast together at his small kitchen table, they didn't exchanged more than a few words before they left the apartment together, he for school, she for her office. Still there was something in the way she had moved about the place—briskly wiping the crumbs from her toast off the table and into her hand, stacking dishes neatly on the counter, raising the milk to her nose to test its potency—that had made him feel at ease, as if all he had denied her was somehow forgotten.

When he returned to his apartment that afternoon he found a brown envelope leaning against his door. Curious, he picked it up and noticed right away it did not have an address or postage on it. There was a scribble note across the back:

> *The cleaner who got the apartment ready for you found these clipped together, on the top shelf of the closet in the bedroom. Not sure how the previous tenants missed them. Anyway, you seemed interested in the story, so I thought I'd pass them along. Enjoy.*

Grady recognized the signature of the realtor who had shown him the apartment. He slid his bag off his shoulder, and standing in front of the locked door, gently tore open the envelope. Inside he found a series of yellowed newspaper clippings. The whole story was there.

In the early 1950s, the Apollo Chamber of Commerce began a tradition that ran for the next nine years. Over the Fourth of July weekend, sections of Water Street were closed off and local merchants were encouraged to sell their wares on the sidewalks. Small, amusement-park-style rides were set up in Chestnut Park. In the late afternoon, the V.F.W. post hosted a chicken barbecue. The festivities culminated in a lavish fireworks display that drew people from as far away as the city of Buffalo.

Sean Rudkowski was just twelve years old the summer of 1959. As evening approached on the Fourth of July, Sean's parents agreed to let him attend the festivities unsupervised. They told him to meet them by the entrance to the park after the fireworks were over.

Initially when Sean failed to show, they assumed it was because he got caught up in the residual excitement of the crowd. Burt Rudkowski stayed to wait for his boy, while his wife went home to see if her only son was there. After an hour, the park was empty and Burt left with a creeping feeling of dread in his belly. The feeling grew as he approached his house and saw his wife sitting alone on the front stoop with a worried expression on her face. After midnight, they called the police.

The town of Apollo held its breath for three days while police organized local men into search teams to scour the area looking for any signs of Sean. There was much speculation as to his whereabouts. Some who had seen him enjoying the rides earlier in the day suggested he might have run off with one of the carnies. In the end, it was a phone call that solved the mystery.

The anonymous man's voice explained that the body of the lost boy could be found in the creek bed behind the storefront apartments on Water Street. The young detective on duty kept the caller on the line long enough to trace the number. Two cars were dispatched, one to fetch the body and one to bring Sam Gregory, the caller, in for questioning.

Nothinh Here is Real

Sean Rudkowski's body was found naked and washing against the rocks of Shenengo creek, exactly where Sam Gregory said it would be. By the time the boy was found he was as white as the underbelly of the catfish that were feeding on him. The multiple puncture wounds in his groin and lower abdomen assured there was almost no blood left in his body.

Sam Gregory was questioned for six hours. He lived with his wife, Thelma, and their son, Ward, in the storefront apartment building behind which the murdered boy's body was found. Sam worked as a clerk at Klinger's, the uptown men's clothing store, and periodically served as an usher at Creekside United Methodist church. As such, he belonged to that group of men who populate small-town America: essential in their own way, but not particularly worthy of notice.

Earlier that spring, Sam Gregory volunteered to coach his son Ward's little league baseball team. Halfway through the season, though, after a series of awkward incidents, the head of Apollo's recreation department intervened and Sam was replaced as the team's coach by a man who better knew his way around bats, gloves, and young boys. Sean Rudkowski was a member of the team.

Chief Hadley was sure Sam Gregory being taken out of his apartment in handcuffs hadn't escaped the notice of his neighbors. Having spent the last three days sleeplessly searching the area for the boy's body with other men from the community, Hadley also knew the people of Apollo were angry and scared and ready to pounce with accusation on the first sniff of suspicion. So after the questioning was over and Sam Gregory was released to his family, Hadley had a squad car escort him home and ordered the officer to stay on the scene until morning, just to be sure nothing out of the ordinary happened.

By 10:00 p.m. a small group of community members, many of whom had been searching for the boy's body, gathered in front of the Gregorys' building. There were no shouts or attempts to ascend the stairs, just people talking about the crime in quiet, convicting voices. The officer's instinct was to break-up the crowd, but to be sure he called the station to report the gathering. Chief Hadley decided to let them stay; get the rumors out of their system he figured, so long as they remain peaceful and don't disturb the family.

The police report later noted that at 10:24 p.m., Sam Gregory appeared behind the curtain of his apartment's front window. The July heat had reached near-record levels that day, but the windows of the Gregorys' apartment had remained closed. When Sam Gregory slowly drew back the curtain and lifted the sash, the collective voice of the crowd below fell silent. He leaned out into the evening air and, backlit by an orange light from within the apartment, looked down on his jury standing below on the street. He stood like this for only a moment before tucking himself back into the apartment and once again closing the window on the outside world. But before he pulled the curtain, the officer noted that the boy, Ward, could be clearly seen standing at his father's side.

Two hours after the lights were turned out in the Gregorys' apartment and the neighbors dispersed into the darkness, Ward Gregory pushed open the front window and showered the sidewalk below with the spilled contents of his stomach. Ward's cries shook awake the officer, who had fallen asleep in the squad car, a cup of coffee in his hand. When the officer could get no intelligible response from the boy as to why he was screaming, he drew his gun and stormed the stairs to the apartment.

Inside, the officer found Sam Gregory slumped in a chair facing the back window that looked out over Shenengo Creek. His wrists were slit and drained.

In the dim light of the hallway, Grady turned the last article over with shaking hands. There he found, written neatly in pencil, a series of brief comments:

> *It must have seemed easier this way. Safer for all of us. They already had their truth. We knew better. But you're the only one who escaped, Papa. Even now, you're the only one who is free.*
> *I forgive you.*

Holding the paper up to the fading light let in by the uncurtained window at the top of the stairs, Grady re-read the penciled note out loud in an awed whisper. At the last phrase, he folded the article neatly and placed it back into the envelope. Opening his bag, he pushed the envelope in, and then walked down the stairs to his car, leaving the apartment door closed and locked behind him.

Grady swung the sedan down Water Street, past the church and headed uptown. He parked his car in front of The Red Newt Art Gallery. The street was silent, and all the lights inside the gallery were off. He got out and looked up at the darkened windows, behind which the lost paintings of Ward Gregory now hung. He shuddered with a new sensation.

Ward Gregory must have known that the living, breathing world isn't good enough for most people. There was a beat in the silence as Grady's thoughts went away, and he heard once again the rise of rushing water and garbled voices in his ears. He shook his head to stop the sounds and climbed back into his car, certain for the first time in his life of the innocence of the artist.

THE STARLING

I was sitting alone, eating a bowl of cold cereal, staring blankly into the silent living room, when I heard it for the first time. THWACK!

At first I thought it was my father working on some project in the basement, trying to distract himself from the reality of what had happened the night before, but a few moments later, I heard it again--a distinct and sudden rap against the silence, like a nail being fruitlessly driven into impenetrable wood. Whatever was making the noise was a stranger to my home.

THWACK! Again it came, sharp and

sudden with a new urgency. I pushed my
breakfast away and began circling the
interior rooms of the house. I took ten
steps, then waited for another volley, so
I might determine where it was coming
from. But whatever it was it had fallen
silent, as if my decision to seek it out
was an invitation to disappear. I was
standing in the living room, listening in
a half-crouch when my father walked in,
still toweling his wet hair.

"Did you hear that?" I asked.

"I was in the shower," he said. "What
did you hear?"

"Something. Sounded like someone
rapping on a window or something."

"It's probably just one of the
neighbors doing chores. You know Mr.
Thompson wouldn't let a Saturday go by
without pounding on something on his
house."

"No, it wasn't that, Dad. It was in
the house."

"Well, whatever it is, I didn't hear
it. Has your mother called?" I shook my

head. It had been almost twelve hours
since either of us had seen her.

"No, she hasn't called. How are we
going to look for her? She took the car."

My father sighed deeply and sat
down on the edge of the table. "I suspect
she went to Ohio to get Emile, but I
don't know really. I suppose I could
borrow your grandfather's car." Then,
cutting himself off, he looked up at me
and sighed again. "Maybe we better talk
this out, Grady," he said, "before we do
anything."

The late news was playing on the TV.
My father and I were sitting mindlessly,
letting the drone of the weatherman's
voice wash over us, when my mother threw
open the bedroom door. The untethered
phone and its ragged, shredded cord
dangled from her fist.

"Are you just going to sit there,
Frank? Just going to sit and watch the
fucking weather?"

"What happened?" my father

stammered back, scrambling out of his
chair to face her.

"What happened? What happened?
Jesus, Frank, haven't you been paying
attention? What happened is Emile is
on the brink of being lost forever, and
you're just sitting here." With that, she
brought the dislodged phone down on the
dining room table with such force that
its hard plastic shell splintered into
pieces across the floor.

"Marty, get a hold of yourself,"
my father said. "Was that Emile on the
phone?"

"No, Frank, that wasn't Emile on the
phone. That was Stephan. My son hangs up
on me, and Stephan calls me back."

"What did he say to you?" My words
seemed to strike both of my parents
unaware, as if all of this was happening
without me in the room.

"Grady, don't you dare judge your
brother. He is sick. It is our job as his
family to help him, and your judgment
has no place..."

"Grady wasn't judging anyone, Marty," my father broke in.

"That's right. That's right, Frank. Drive a wedge between my other son and me. It worked out so great with the first one, didn't it?"

"What are you talking about, Marty?"

"What am I talking about?" She threw his question back at him. "Emile just had to go to your precious alma mater, didn't he? Just had to follow in Daddy Dearest's footsteps."

"That was his decision."

"His decision? Honestly, Frank, do you know your son at all? Do you honestly think without your prodding Emile would have chosen to move seven hours away? Because I don't think so. I don't think my son is the type of person who would decide, after two weeks of knowing some homosexual from Bethlehem, Pennsylvania, to cast his mother aside like so much trash."

"Emile and this kid are trying to get a campus radio show off the ground,

Marty. That takes a lot of time. And don't forget he's got classes on top of that."

"Don't talk to me like I never went to school, Frank. You're the one who barely graduated." She stormed into the kitchen and reached for the other phone. "You know, this is exactly what I'm talking about. I'm glad you and Emile finally decided to act like father and son after all of these years. It's great you sat him down and told him all about your college experiences, but I won't be cast aside like I'm nothing, Frank, not after all that I've given that boy, and certainly not in the name of some rinky-dink campus radio show, or some fairy from Pennsylvania." She picked up the phone and began to dial Emile's number.

"Marty, I know you're upset, but please..."

"Please what, Frank? Please stop? Is that what you're going to ask me to do? Well, forget it, okay? I'm not going to stop. Not when my child is in danger."

"What's going on?" my father

pleaded.

She slammed the phone back down into its cradle, "Your son's new friend--and that's how he introduced himself to me--had the audacity to call this house and tell me to stay out of my son's life. He told me to 'cut the umbilical cord.'"

"He said that to you?"

"No, Frank, I'm making it up, okay? You just go back to your eleven o'clock news while I try to hold what's left of this family together."

The phone suddenly sprang to life. My mother spun away from my father and me and yanked the receiver off the hook. "Emile?"

My father and I glanced quickly at each other and rushed into the kitchen, lest she do anything drastic with our one remaining phone.

"How dare he speak to me that way!" she screamed into the receiver.

"Marty!" My father reached for her.

"Get away from me, Frank, I swear to God."

Nothing Here is Real

"Marty, calm down. Let me talk to Emile."

My mother was holding the phone to her ear while screaming at my father. "You've done enough already, Frank." She turned her back to us and began speaking furtively. "Emile, I know you're confused, I know things seem dark right now, but that boy had no right to call this house.

"No, sweetheart, I want you to have friends.

"But you've just met this boy. How could you possibly know that?

"I'm not sure you know what you are asking of me, Emile, but I will not stand idly by while you throw away everything you've ever known about right and wrong." Her tone was shifting back toward rage.

"How can you say that to me? How dare you say that to me? Is that homosexual in the room with you right now?" My father wrenched the phone from my mother's hands.

"Emile, what's going on?" my father barked into the phone. Like a wild

animal, my mother's hands were on my
father's face. He spun away in a vain
effort to maintain his conversation
with my brother. Hunched over with his
hips against my mother's raging form, he
fended her off as he spoke inaudibly into
the receiver. My mother lunged and dug
at him, striking his back in a pantomime
of frustration and childish rage.
Suddenly, my father stopped struggling
and stood up fully to face my mother. She
grabbed the phone.

"Emile, your father... Emile?"

"He's hung up, Marty," my father
said.

She stood staring at my father, the
dial tone echoing out of the earpiece.

"Marty, we have to let him be."

"No, Frank, that's just where you're
wrong." Then, as if interrupted by a
thought, "Let him be what? This Stephan,
this new friend of Emile's? Is that what
you mean? Well, I didn't give my whole
life to that child to have him turn
toward some predatory homosexual the

first month he's away at college."

"Marty, you're jumping to conclusions. I've told you that a hundred times."

"Did you listen to the phone conversation, Frank?"

"You know I didn't."

"Then you don't know what I heard. This is a sick and disturbed child, and he's poisoning Emile." Her voice trailed off as tears sprang to her eyes. Suddenly, she spun away from my father and me, her hands scattering the unwashed dinner dishes onto the kitchen floor.

"You can just forget it, Frank, this whole little fantasy-The Picketts of Apollo," she spat the words. "It's all just a load of bullshit."

"Marty, stop and think about what you're saying. Grady is right here." My mother looked at me blinking back at her.

"And how long will it be, Grady, before you treat me like shit? Before you tell me I'm a terrible mother? Before you turn your back on everything we ever taught you is right? How long?"

I stared at her silently.

"I asked you a fucking question!"

"Marty!"

"No, Frank, I want to know. I have a right to ask."

"Mom, I..."

"Grady," my father interrupted me, "go to your room. This doesn't concern you."

"That's right, Grady, you run away and hide. No need to be a part of the family," my mother taunted.

"That's enough, Marty!" my father snapped. "You're out of control."

He reached for her, but she whirled toward the counter and unsheathed the carving knife from the wooden block next to the toaster. She held her left wrist up to the light and moved to run the naked blade against it. My father was upon her in an instant and broke her grasp on the knife, sending it skittering across the kitchen floor as he wrenched away the offending hand.

Nothing Here is Real

For a moment she stood stock
still like a chastised child caught
in the throes of some unspeakable act
of disobedience. I was standing on the
threshold between the kitchen and the
back door, close enough to my mother to
see the mist of spittle that clung to the
delicate hairs on her upper lip.

With unnatural movements, she
jerked her hand free from my father's
grasp and swiped her keys from the hook
by the door. Then she stumbled toward me
in a blind rage.

"Get out of my way. I have to get out
of here."

"Marty, stop. Will you look at your
child?" I stepped toward her and reached
out to grab her shoulders. In an instant,
she scrambled by me. I turned to see her
looking back through the closing glass.
Her eyes were wild with a living hatred
that paralyzed my movements.

My father brushed past me, but by
the time he got to her, she had locked
the car door and started the engine. His

arresting cries were inaudible over the
roar of the car. And then she was gone.

"What happened last night had
nothing to do with you," my father
said. "You know that, right?" I nodded
wordlessly. "Your mother is just upset."

"But what is she upset about?"

"Emile is just..." He was silent for
a moment, searching for how to begin.
"Emile is trying to figure out who he is."

"Is Mom worried Emile is gay, Dad? I
mean, is that what Mom is so upset about?"

"Grady, Emile and your mother have
a special relationship. They've always
been very close. Emile never really had
many friends, so when he latched on to
this Stephan guy... your mother is just
jumping to conclusions. She means well.
She just wants you boys to be happy."

Again I was silent. I walked back
over to address the dregs of my soggy
cereal. Then, looking directly at my
father, I said, "It didn't seem like she
meant well in the kitchen last night,

Dad."

My father looked away. After the car left he had come back into the house. We had barely spoken. He had picked up the knife and tossed it into the sink, then after taking a few steps away he returned to the basin and flipped the hot water on with the back of his hand. He squirted a line of dish soap on the blade and began to needlessly rinse it off. "Go to bed, Grady" was all he said.

"Grady, your mother was upset."

"I know, Dad, but I get upset all the time, and you don't see me reaching for the cutlery."

"That's enough," my father said.

"But, I just think..."

"I said, that's enough." Then, rising he added, "We'll not speak of that again."

THWACK! Both of us stopped.

"That's the sound I heard before you came downstairs," I said.

THWACK! THWACK!

"It seems like it's coming from the basement," my father said.

The stairs to the basement were
behind the door off the dining room.
We opened it, switched on the light,
and proceeded down them together. The
basement looked as it always did--a
mixture of cobwebs, mildew stained walls,
and piles of unfinished laundry heaped
in front of the washing machine. "It
stopped."

"It did the same thing before, when
you came downstairs. I heard it when I
was eating breakfast, but when I got up
to look for it, it just stopped."

My father pointed at the ground.
"What the hell is that?" We both looked
and saw a small pile of debris gathered
at the base of the chimney.

I kneeled down and scooped some of
it up in my hand. "These are ashes, Dad."
Then, letting my eyes scan up the face
of the chimney, I saw a small, iron door
slightly ajar. "This door's kinda open.
The ashes must have blown out of that."

My father stepped around me to
close it, but suddenly jumped back with a

yelp. "Get away from there, Grady!"

I scurried up a few steps of the stairs, and when my father moved out of the light coming in through the glass block windows, I saw what had startled him.

THWACK! THWACK! A small black wing suddenly thrust itself into the space between the open iron door and the exterior wall of the chimney. THWACK! THWACK!

"There's a bird trapped in there. Get the laundry basket."

My father put the laundry basket over the opening, then flipped the iron door open with an old stirring stick he found on top of some leftover paint cans. Out of the darkness, a small black bird stared back at us.

"It's a starling," my father said in a whisper. "See its yellow beak?" I nodded. "It must have been sitting at the top of the chimney and got overwhelmed with fumes."

"Why isn't it moving?" I asked.

"It's probably just stunned. It'll
move once it discovers it's free." And
then as if on command, the bird burst
violently from the chimney door, headlong
into the plastic laundry basket. My
father yelped again and dropped the
basket onto the floor. Having thrown
itself into the basket with the force of
desperate escape, the bird looked up at
us, frozen in a blind daze.

"Cover it up, Dad, before it moves
again!"

My father turned and yanked free a
sheet hanging from the clotheslines that
was draped from the low-slung ceiling of
the basement, sending clothespins flying
in crazy directions all over the room.
Then he threw it over the basket. "Let's
get this guy outside, where he belongs."

"Wait," I said. "I think there's
something else in there."

The small door at the base of the
chimney stood open on rusted hinges.
In the basement's light, I saw clumps
of shapes inside the box-like space. I

crouched down on a knee, opened the
door fully, and saw what the starling
must have only sensed: the bottom of my
parents' chimney was a tomb. Small piles
of bones and dusty feathers littered the
lightless space. With the door now open,
the stench of decay was overwhelming.
"Jesus," I whispered. "There must be at
least three other bodies down here."

"Leave the bodies for later," my
father said. "This one's still alive."

We walked together with the covered
basket to the edge of the driveway and
set it down on the flat corner post of
the otherwise picketed fence lining the
yard. Stepping away he pulled the sheet
gingerly from the basket, exposing the
starling to its freedom.

"Do you think it's still in shock?" I
said.

"Give it a minute." We stood
together, wordlessly watching the bird.

The honk of the car's horn made us
both jump, as my mother pulled the family

sedan into the driveway. She stopped in front of us with the window down.

"Why are the two of you standing there looking at the laundry basket on the fence?" she asked.

"We're setting the starling free," I said.

"I don't follow you."

"It was stuck in the chimney in the basement. We're setting it free."

"Well," she smiled awkwardly indicating the empty basket with her eyes, "mission accomplished." Then she pulled the car forward without further acknowledgement of either my father or me.

I was instructed to go into the basement and finish cleaning up the mess created by the starling's escape, so my parents might have some time alone to talk. When their voices fell silent, the door to the basement opened, and my mother descended the stairs. Her face was red and streaked with tears. Before I could say anything, she sat down on the second-to-last step and patted the empty space next to her. "Come here. We need to talk."

I shuffled over from my father's workbench where I had been busying myself organizing old soup cans of mismatched nails into coherent piles on the broad and sanded surface. "I'm sorry about last night, Grady," she said, her voice catching. "I just got overwhelmed with everything. Everything that's been going on." I nodded.

"After I left here last night, I drove to Ohio to get your brother. To bring him home. It was around 5:00 a.m. when I got there. I went straight to Emile's dorm and found someone had propped open the door with a pizza box." She was talking into space, not even attempting to look me in the eyes. "At first, no one answered when I knocked. To be honest, I was expecting his roommate Ralph to answer." My mother cleared her throat and wiped a tear from her

eye with the back of her hand before
she continued. "But it wasn't Ralph who
answered the door."

"Was it Emile?" I asked.

"No, it was another boy. A dark-
skinned boy. I believe he is from India.
His name is Stephan. He is a friend of
your brother's."

"Was Emile there?"

"Of course he was. When he heard
my voice he came into the hall and
agreed to take a walk with me. We walked
around campus, and I explained to him my
concerns--how I feel he is deliberately
trying to disown this family, to excluded
us from his life."

"And what did he say?"

"Well, that's what I want to talk to
you about, Grady. See, Emile told me some
very troubling things, things I simply
can't let go without taking some action."

"What did he tell you?"

"I explained to him my concern
about what I perceived to be his...
shall we say, 'relationship' with this

Indian boy, Stephan. He assured me that
the distance he's been keeping from the
family has nothing to do with anything
related to this boy, but rather because of
the general sense of alienation he feels
from your father."

"What?"

She paused now, and I could sense
a shift in her tone. "There is no excuse
for the way for the way your father has
treated your brother all these years. I
see that now, in a way I simply couldn't
have seen it before." I stood silently and
shifted my feet to face her. She raised
her hand before I could speak.

"There is no need to try to defend
your father. He has agreed to the
separation."

"The separation? What?"

"Yes, your father is going to go live
with your uncle, while he and I try to
work on our marriage."

"What the fuck, Mom?" I blurted out.

"I can understand why you're upset.
This certainly is unsettling for all of

us, honey, but believe me when I tell you,
it's far worse for me than it is for you."

"Does Emile know about this?"

"Yes. I told him my plans."

"What did he say?"

"He was concerned, mostly because of
the impact all of this would have on you.
He loves you very much, you know. But I
think he finally came to understand this
is my only choice. To save the family, I
have to let your father know his actions
are unacceptable."

"What actions?" I pleaded.

"You don't know everything about
your father, Grady. Every marriage has
its secrets, and some of them are simply
unforgivable. You're old enough to know
that now."

"This is crazy, Mom. You drive all
the way to Ohio after storming out of
here like you did, talk to Emile for half
an hour, then decide to turn everyone's
life upside down, and you can't even tell
me what's really going on?"

"How selfish can you be, Grady?

Nothing Here is Real

Really, I know you've always favored your
father over me, but honest to God, have
you thought for even one second about
how all of this is affecting me?" Her
eyes filled with tears. "I am your mother,
after all. Did it ever occur to you that I
might need some comforting?"

"Why does Dad have to leave? Just
last night you were upstairs screaming
about Emile..."

"I didn't know that whole story
then, Grady."

"What, about Stephan, Mom?"

"I met the boy face to face. I know
my son. Even if Emile is gay--which he's
not--he would never go for a boy like
that."

"I can't believe this. Where's Dad?"

"Haven't you been listening? He's
gone to your uncle's. We'll start couple's
counseling on Monday. Emile will be home
next weekend."

"What? Emile is coming home?"

"Yes. For the weekend, yes. That
was one stipulation I made before I left

there. He'll catch the bus after his late
class on Thursday."

"Will Dad be here?"

"We'll see how Monday's session goes."
She stood and draped her arms around
me. "Listen, I love you, Grady. I want the
best for you. I know you must be confused
now, but believe me when I tell you this
is for the best."

"I can't believe Dad just left,"
I said, brushing past her and up the
stairs. "He didn't even say good-bye."

"I didn't give him a choice, Grady,"
she called up after me. "I didn't give him
a choice."

Five days later, as a stunning cold
front blew over the lake and brought
with it a heavy dose of early snow, my
brother came home from college for the
first time. He was sitting alone at the
dining room table when I walked into the
house after school.

"Hey," he said.

"I thought you weren't going to be

here till later," I replied. "Mom said you were taking the bus."

"Nice to see you, too. And I did take the bus, just an earlier one than expected. I took a cab home from the city. Don't worry, I called mom at work and told her she didn't need to pick me up." I slid my backpack onto the kitchen counter and opened up the refrigerator.

"I know I took you by surprise there, but shit, I'm your brother." He walked over to me and lamely wrapped his arms around me. When I moved to step away, his embraced lingered. "What's going on, Grady?" he asked. "Tell me what's really going on."

I pushed away from him. "I don't know, Emile. You tell me."

"You're blaming me for this?"

"All I know is that Mom comes home from Ohio, and suddenly Dad's living at Uncle Gary's house. You do the math."

Emile turned his head away and laughed falsely. "Not everything is that simple, okay?"

"Right. I'm sure there's some grand explanation that's beyond my understanding, right?"

"Actually, there is," Emile said. "Why don't you take a walk with me, and I'll tell you about it?"

"It's cold as hell out there, Emile. And besides, Mom will be pissed if she comes home and finds you aren't here."

Emile grabbed my forearm. Tears were welling in his eyes when I turned to face him. "Grady, please. I've got to talk to somebody. I have to get this off my chest."

"So talk. Why do we need to walk somewhere?"

"I want to go to the woods," Emile said. "Please."

"Fine," I said, and grabbed my coat.

The sky had darkened and even though the wind had calmed considerably the snow continued to fall at a steady clip. Determined not to be the first one to speak, I walked with Emile in silence

across the schoolyard, under the lights
of the building and toward the dark
shadow of Worthingdale Woods. Suddenly,
I no longer felt him by my side.

I turned to find he was kneeling
in the snow ten yards behind me. The
security lights from the school switched
on and cast my brother in a long shadow
that reached toward me in the now almost-
full darkness of the October afternoon.

When I was next to him, he looked
up at me with the tears streaming down
his face, his hands folded in a posture
of prayer, his body rocking gently. "Pray
with me, Grady. Please God, pray with me."

"I'm here," I said.

His hand reached up and he pulled
me down next to him in the snow. We knelt
together twenty yards from the building,
in the middle of the windswept expanse
that stretched between the school and the
woods.

"God, help me." Emile said, his eyes
now closed and his hands still folded
before him. "I have to confess to somebody

I can trust. Somebody I know will never say anything."

I was silent. "Can I trust you to never say a word about what I am about to tell you?"

My only reply was silence. After a minute, Emile began to speak. "I've been pledging this fraternity--Chi Sigma Nu. This buddy of mine, Stephan, and I are pledging together. I haven't said anything about it to Mom and Dad, so they're all freaked out about me hanging out with him so much."

"Why don't you just tell them why you're always with this guy, and then they'll get off your back?"

Emile looked at me in the darkness. "Because before I left for school, Dad swore he wouldn't help me with tuition if I decided to pledge. He doesn't give a shit about anything, unless you do it his way. So I made up some lie about starting a radio show, because I knew Dad did something like that when he was there. Shit, I don't even know if the school

still has a radio station, but I figured
that'd get them off my back anyway. But
it only made things worse.

"This one time I was out with
Stephan and didn't call home when I
said I would. Mom flipped out. She got it
in her head I was turning gay. I mean,
that's just bullshit. She just doesn't
understand--Stephen and I kind of
have to hang out a lot if we hope to be
brothers, but I couldn't tell Mom that."

"Why are we praying?" I asked, self-
conscious of the conversation that seemed
to contradict our postures. But as I moved
to stand, Emile clutched my shoulder.

"Please, pray, Grady. Pray for me."

"For what, for God's sake?" I asked.

"I told Stephan about what Mom
said--how she thought we were gay--and
then he freaked out, too. He told me I
should call her and tell her to fuck
off, but I wouldn't call. We were drunk.
I didn't know what I might say. So he
started talking like maybe Mom was
right, maybe I am gay. I didn't want

him to go to the other brothers with the
story. But when I denied it, he told me to
prove it, or else he'd tell everyone I was
a fag. So that's what I did."

"What does that mean?" I asked.

"It means I fucked this girl,
Dorothy Cassidy," he said in a choked
voice. "She's kind of the frat house whore.
Most of the brothers have hooked up with
her. There aren't sororities there, so I
guess the way she sees it, 'Membership
has its privileges.' At least that's what
she said to me after we finished." Emile's
eyes remained closed as he spoke to the
darkness.

Swallowing my repulsion, I said,
"So you had sex with a fraternity whore.
Worse things could happen."

He jerked into an upright position
and grabbed the collars of my jacket.
"Grady, God, worse things have happened.
Fuck! Dorothy thinks she might be
pregnant."

"Jesus." I stared at my brother's
twisted face.

Nothing Here is Real

"She swears I'm the only guy she's been with since the last time she was on the rag."

"Shit, Emile."

"I tried to stop her, but she's going to have an abortion. There's nothing I can do." I said nothing in reply.

"Promise me you won't say anything, Grady. Swear to me."

"I promise," I said.

"It's not my fault. Can't you see that?" he begged, but I didn't answer him. "You've got to pray for me, Grady. Pray for all of us."

So there in the snowfield next to my elementary school, I pretended to pray as my brother rocked back and forth, muttering words to the darkness. I wrapped my arms around him and helped him to his feet. On the way home, I once again swore to never speak a word of what he shared.

It is an oath I have never broken. Not during that weekend, through the tense meals and long walks I endured with my family as my brother carried out his elaborate radio-station lie. Not at Christmastime when Emile returned home from school with a transcript of three Fs and a D, the contents of his dorm room, and a letter from the dean mandating that he take an indefinite "leave of absence" from the school until "course work completed at an outside, and comparable, institution of higher learning demonstrates he has the focus to be the type of student he was expected to be when granted a letter of admission." Not even that night in early April, when Emile took Stephan's call in his bedroom, then rushed out of the door in a rage. Even then, I was silent.

I held my tongue when the ambulance sirens pierced the spring evening, when the call came and my mother fell to the floor, when my father picked up the dangling receiver and was told by a state trooper that when the car hit the tree at seventy miles per hour, Emile's body was thrown through

Nothing Here is Real

the windshield. My father wept into his
hands in the kitchen like a child. Even
then, I never said a word about Dorothy
Cassidy.

Later, a man from the insurance
company came to the house and spoke
to my parents about the results of the
investigation. In all the following
years, I remained silent about that, too.
What was there to say really about an
accident without any skid marks?

- G. Pickett
Apollo, NY - November 16, 2010

MYTHS

1.

The Red Newt Art Gallery's late-October opening drew a larger than expected crowd. Anita Kennedy was savvy in her marketing of the evening, slowly leaking hints about what it was she planned to reveal in the papers and by word of mouth, so by the time the evening came, it had evolved into a full-fledged event. The three major Buffalo television stations were on the scene, as were The Buffalo News, The Apollo Sun, and several other local papers from towns in the surrounding areas. What Anita Kennedy didn't expect were protestors.

An hour before the gallery opened, Emile Pickett and 12 other members of the Vita Coalition arrived, dressed in black with signs and bullhorns, and promptly began marching in a circle across the street from the front door. When the reporters asked what the group's objection to the gallery was, Emile Pickett spoke directly to the cameras.

"The artist whose work will be on display tonight, took his own life. The Vita Coalition believes in the Bible and the words of Jesus Christ, both of which condemn suicide as a sin. We reject the idea that such a man should be celebrated—especially when one considers these paintings were recovered after his death.

"The driving force behind the Vita Coalition is to lift up the value of life. We've made a name for ourselves outside of the murder houses that are the abortion clinics of this state. We see our work here this evening as an extension of that."

Then raising his voice Emile shouted across the street at the growing crowd, "So we're here to ask anyone who goes through those doors tonight what they might say to the family of a child who takes his own life in a distorted attempt to become the next celebrated artist of Apollo."

Though the camera and notebooks eventually turned away, Emile's voice was an incessant rebuke of each person who entered the gallery. "You want the children of this town to die for fame, Bill? How can you fly in the face of the scriptures, Katie, when you attend mass each week?" Emile stood as his fellow Coalition members circled around him, singing dirges and carrying signs carefully covered with scripture.

Grady arrived after the initial thrust of the crowd thinned out. He walked the half-mile uptown to where the gallery was located, next to the Masonic temple. As he approached the door, Emile saw him, and for the first time

in an hour, fell silent. In fact none of the members of the
Vita Coalition spoke or moved for the ten minutes it took
for Grady to gain entry into the building.

Grady had seen his brother at a distance and
swore to himself that he wouldn't engage him. Still, on the
threshold of the gallery Grady glanced across the street and
saw that Emile's eyes had never left him. Stirred by their
shared gaze, Emile raised a megaphone to his mouth and
began to speak. But then the door closed, and Emile's voice
was washed out by the excited murmur of the gallery's
crowd.

Grady was unable to move when he saw them,
unable to reconcile the sensation of sight with the
possibility of circumstance. The visions of Ward Gregory
on display before him defied reality in such a way that the
room seemed to morph into a cavern in which Grady felt
himself drawn toward the images at the end of a tunnel of
light.

The first painting, complete in all aspects save the
fulfillment of what looked to be a building scaffolded in
rough strokes on the right side of the canvas, was a winter
scene. The snow fell heavily, blurring the nighttime sky to
the point that the painting was devoid of celestial light.
The face of the young man in the center of the painting,

kneeling in a desperate posture of prayer, was obscured by shadows, backlit only by the distant floodlights of the building. Still, the identity of the boy was unmistakable— Grady knew him at once.

The second painting depicted a slope in a deeply shaded wood. It might have been any worn trail, but Grady recognized something in it that told him more. To anyone else, those were slants of light piercing the canopy of trees, but Grady saw them as the contaminated spikes of Emile's trip-wire trap; it was the gully of the water war. The painting emerged upward from where the deer laid impaled. Grady followed the sight lines up the canvas to where he saw Emile first emerge from the shadows, framed by the wings of the turkey vultures. The rendered image wove the fibers of Grady's memory together into a living thing, and he forced himself to look away, lest the fawn and its mirrored, lifeless eyes appear before him as well.

The last of the paintings was titled, The Marrow. It was surreal in its incompletion. What was clear on the canvas was a stretch of trees on either side of a central passageway. The trees were naked of leaves, but still their dense branches formed a semi-canopy over the unfinished center of the piece. From what Grady could tell, if the image had been brought to wholeness, it would have revealed itself to be a lonely stretch of tree-lined road, shimmering in the twilight sky. He experienced this painting most blindly, for of the three, it was the only one whose subject he had not experienced directly.

Grady staggered away from the paintings and into the arms of Crosby Gibbons, who was clearly drunk or stoned or quite possibly both. "What'd I tell you, huh?" Gibby offered. "She's found the real deal." There was a remarkably beautiful woman on Crosby's arm who was smiling broadly back at Grady. At first, Grady mistook the old man's comment as a boast about the unearthly creature by his side, until a puzzled look from Crosby brought him back to his senses. "Grady Pickett, meet Anita Kennedy." The two of them shook hands.

"My God," the woman said, "your hand feels like a block of ice. Not only that but all the color is gone from your lips."

"You'll have to forgive me," Grady started.

"Does he always look this way, Crosby? Forgive me. Are you ill?"

"No, no, I'm fine. It's only that I've just seen them," he said, pointing over his shoulder at the paintings.

"Anita's right there, buddy. You look like shit." Gibby cuffed Grady on the shoulder, a blow that nearly sent him tumbling to the floor. Grady gathered himself and walked away without responding, stumbling toward the exit, down the stairs, and into the cold October night.

The Vita Coalition had moved across the street when Grady emerged from the gallery. Doing his best to ignore them, he gulped the cold night air hoping it would help his feet once again feel as though they belonged to his body. Aside from the shouts of the Vita Coalition, the street seemed quite and empty juxtaposed with the shoulder-to-shoulder crowd inside the gallery. As Grady turned to leave, Emile grabbed his shoulder and spun Grady around to face him.

The violence of the gesture betrayed the calmness in Emile's face. "What's up, Emile?" Grady said.

"Grady, listen, I was talking with Sarah earlier tonight. Trying to come up with a plan for what to do if I saw you here."

"Well I'm glad you came prepared."

"It's because of her that I didn't call you out as you walked in there tonight. She made me realize I was wrong to think of shaming you."

"Shaming me?"

"I came here tonight to tell everyone within ear shot what I believe in my heart—Ward Gregory is an evil force in this world. I knew that if I saw you entering that gallery to celebrate his work I would feel betrayed all over again."

"Betrayed? What are you talking about?"

"How could you do that, Grady? How could you want anything to do with that man after what he did to our family?"

"What did he do to our family, Emile?"

"Is it possible you've forgotten?"

"Emile, I remember everything, but..."

"Then there is no 'but' about it. If you remember, that's enough to confirm my worst suspicion."

"And what might that be?"

"That evil has you in its grasp."

"You really have lost your shit, do you know that?"

"Grady." Emile grabbed his brother's arm. "Stop. It's okay. I will help you. Come with me. Come with me to St. Adalbert's. Sarah is right. We can't cast you aside. There is always hope in Christ. Come with us. It's never too late."

"Get your fucking hands off me!" Grady said, and pulled out of his brother's grip. "You can sell your crazy talk to your clones, but don't sell it here. I saw those paintings..." As he spoke, Grady turned and saw for the first time that the rest of the Vita Coalition had stopped marching and now stood watching the exchange.

"Don't talk to me about those paintings!" Emile

cried.

"Emile, that man painted things, vivid images of things, that happened after he died. You want to explain that?"

"Don't talk to me about that man! His life is worthless. He means nothing to me."

"Oh, that's nice. I'm so sorry, Emile. Forgive me for assuming you saw Ward Gregory as a human being. Because that's what he was. A sad, fucked-up human being. Forgive me for mentioning him. I was still feeling moved by the whole 'value of life' act you and the other assholes in black were pulling earlier tonight."

"You want to talk about hypocrisy? Fine. Let's do that." Emile's eyes were ablaze with passion. "Hypocrisy is standing up at town meetings pretending to care about the life of deer when in reality all you want to do is rub my face in shit from the past. Hypocrisy is going to galleries and weeping over art created by a man who raped your family and stole your brother's life. That's all fine. You can do that if you want, but let me tell you this, Grady–you have no right, no right, to talk to me about the value of life. You who were willing to kill your own child."

The words hung in the air between them.

Grady took a step back and stared at his brother, his eyes suddenly stinging. "You have no idea what you're talking about, Emile," Grady said, in a strained voice.

"I know what happened, and so do you. Do you think the seal on your little world of hate is so tight God's light can't shine in? All of our statistics tell us that one in four unplanned pregnancies end in abortion. But not yours, right? No, I'm sure you and your unwed girlfriend just lost your baby? Right. Sure, that's what happened. Well, you can try to sell your bullshit sob story to Mom and Dad, but I know the truth, Grady."

The first blow split Emile's lips and sent him crashing backwards to the pavement. Grady was upon him in a second and sent his fists flying blindly against Emile's nose, his eyes, his ears. Emile frantically tried to escape, but Grady's weight was too much for him; the blows kept coming. With his knees in his brother's back, Grady twisted Emile's hair in his hand and began to thrust Emile face against the cold surface of the pavement. Grady felt nothing but the absolute bliss of rage.

Then Grady felt an explosion in his head. The blunt end of the two-by-four on which a sign was nailed hit him squarely in the throat. He tumbled off Emile, grasping his neck in pain. The man who struck him dropped the sign and turned to help Emile. Grady lay prone and dazed on the ground, clutching his throat and gasping for breath. He saw a shoe coming toward his face. Then a flash of light.

Nothing Here is Real

Then nothing.

Before the photographer from the paper could snap a picture, the police wrestled Grady to his feet. By the time the camera clicked its front-page photo, Emile had grabbed his sign and was holding it behind his brother. "God chose life," the sign read. The caption below explained the rest.

Susan Luster was sitting with her mother, watching the evening news in astonishment when her cell phone rang. She looked at the screen to see who was calling, then put the receiver to her ear.

"Hey, Sue. It's Grady Pickett."

"That's funny. The caller ID said this was the Apollo Police station."

"Yeah, that's kinda why I'm calling. How's your case load these days?"

"Why do you ask, Grady?"

"Well, it's a long story, but let's just say, you're my one phone call. I'm in here on assault charges."

"I know. I was just watching the news with my mom. They led with the story of a fight at a local art gallery. Your brother looked pretty beat up, but they got an interview out of him anyway."

"It was on the news?"

"Well what did you think would happen, Grady? Jesus Christ! What possessed you to do this?"

"Susan, look, I appreciate your concern and all, but to be honest, right now I'd like to get the hell out of here. Is there any chance you could come bail me out, so I don't have to spend the night?"

"You are such a piece of work, you know that?" she snapped. "You not only think I have time to take on your silly case, but you've also got the gall to ask me to come bail you out." She hung up the phone. Grady was led back to the holding cell. He sat on an iron cot with his back against the wall.

They had used nine stitches to close the gash on his cheek opened by the protestor's kick. The searing pain in back of his neck still felt like an untended fire, but he had been processed and was finally lying down. The ceiling of the room swirled before his eyes. He slid one foot off the cot to steady himself against the feeling of drunkenness. He could think of nothing but the spinning and his need for it to stop. Despite the noise of the station, he kept his eyes tightly shut, and a few minutes later, a sense of stillness settled over his body. He fell into a dreamless sleep.

He awoke to the cell being slid open. When he sat up, Grady saw his father framed by the glow of the overhead lights. They looked at each other silently and in mutual fascination. It was a moment before either man spoke.

"You look awful," Frank said to his son.

"What are you doing here, Dad?"

"Well, your friend Susan called. She said you needed someone to bail you out."

"She's a nice girl."

"Seems like it." His father rubbed his forehead softly, and then said, "Anyway, your mother is down at the hospital with Emile. We were watching the news. She and Sarah left just as I was finishing up the dishes. That's when your friend called."

"I know this seems pretty bad, Dad."

"It doesn't seem bad, Grady; it is bad." Frank fingered the wattle hanging from his chin. "I wish there was something I could say to you, but there just isn't. There's just no way to make it right, Grady."

"Then why come?"

"I'm not bailing you out, if that's what you're thinking."

"What?"

"I've wanted to talk to you for a long time. There are just a few things I want to understand."

"And you figured I've got time to kill so why not

come ask me now?"

"Pretty much, yeah."

"This is unbelievable. Did you tell the cops that?"

"You seem to be taking this whole thing pretty lightly," his father snapped at him, now openly frustrated. "You're in a shitload of trouble."

"Well, what am I supposed to do, wail myself hoarse in the cell at the injustice of it all? It is what it is."

"Injustice?"

"Yeah, that's right, injustice," Grady spat back at his father. "It's a crime that I'm sitting in this jail cell, while my asshole brother is outside spinning stories about me on the news."

Frank paced across the floor, then stood with his back to his son, his head lowered, his right hand rubbing the back of his neck. He swung around. "You know, Grady, I never understood what went wrong with the two of you. Did you see what you did to Emile's face? He's your brother. I mean, when I look at pictures of you two from when you were kids; you guys were like peas in a pod."

"Memory is a great myth-maker, Dad," Grady shot back at him.

"What does that mean?"

"You tell yourself these bullshit stories so many times that you start to believe them. Here are the facts:

nothing ever went wrong to change things between Emile and me. This is the way it's always been."

"Our family was always close. There's no myth about that."

"Really, Dad? Then what about the time Mom kicked you out of the house? What about Emile's accident? What about all of that, huh?" Grady was shouting now.

"Why are you so angry?"

"I'm angry because Emile is trying to highjack my life with bullshit stories, and now you're doing it too. Look, you're free to remember the past anyway you'd like, but don't impose your fucked up reality on me. I know the truth."

Grady looked up at his father who was standing before him, his face contorted with pain. "Dad, I'm not saying all of it was bad, but some of it was, okay?" Grady waited, but his father didn't respond. "It's just you and Mom…you want to remember everything as perfect, but nothing is perfect, Dad. When you pretend it was, you create this unrealistic expectation for how things should be—like we all have to find some way to *make things right* again."

"What's wrong with wanting to make things right?" his father asked earnestly.

"Because you're trying to recreate something

that never existed in the first place." Grady sat down exasperated. "And that's dangerous."

"Dangerous?"

"Yeah, dangerous. It starts by mis-remembering stories about quaint pictures, and the next thing you know, it's like the past is some ball of clay in your hands to mold to suit your needs. Well, I don't care what Emile says. I know what happened to my family, and that's good enough for me."

"You mean our family," his father corrected.

"No. I'm talking about Briarly and my daughter. Just because somebody chooses not to believe the truth doesn't make it any less true."

The police officer standing at the door to the cell cleared his throat. "Frank Pickett?"

"Yes."

"Your wife is holding on the line."

Frank left with the officer, and Grady paced the cell, waiting for his father to return. When he heard the door at the end of the hall open, Grady squeezed his face through the bars and looked as far as he could down the hallway. His father was still a ways away when he called out, "Emile is dropping the charges." Grady took a step back.

"So I'm free to go."

Nothing Here is Real

The officer cleared his throat. "There's some paper work to fill out." Frank was standing silently in the hall next to his son and the officer. "This way, please," the officer said. Grady looked at his father and without saying another word, followed the cop down the hall. After filling out the required forms, Grady was released. Frank waited in the hall, and when he was sure his son would be fine, he drove home. Grady walked back to his apartment alone.

2.

After he left school the following morning, he went back to the apartment and called Susan.

"What is it?" she asked.

"Emile dropped the charges, but I was put on administrative leave this morning anyway. But that's not why I'm calling. I've got something I want you to take a look at."

"I leave for work soon."

"Can I bring it over now? I mean, can you wait until I get there to leave?"

"What is it, Grady?"

"It's just something you need to see. Please."

"Fine," she said. Then she hung up the phone.

He turned on the computer and called up the chapters he'd been working on since late in the summer. He printed them off without reading them over. He had just enough paper to finish the job. He clipped them together in separate sections and stacked them in chronological order. Before stuffing the papers inside a large envelope he wrote the title of each piece across the top of its first page. The Artist. Water War. The Starling. Then he sealed the enveloped, tucked it under his arm, and headed across town to give his story to Susan.

He pulled the sedan to the curb in front of her apartment and as he walked to the door, he picked up the newspaper that was resting at the end of the driveway. He carried the paper in one hand, his writing in the other. When he reached the door he pushed the bell with his thumb.

She was dressed for the day, her hair still slightly wet, and was working an earring into its place when she met him at the door. "Jesus, your face is a mess. Come in," she said and turned back inside. He followed her but stopped just a few feet into the place. Susan walked to the kitchen and stood by the sink finishing the last of her orange juice.

"Your mom's not up yet?"

"She's up. She just likes to lie in bed for a while listening to the scanner before she eats. You said you had something to show me? I assume you didn't come here to talk about my mother."

"Susan, obviously you're angry. I know I owe you an explanation."

"No, I'm just running late for work," she called out over her shoulder without looking at him. "And you don't owe me anything, Grady. You've got your life to live, and I've got mine." She walked toward him, then turned into the half-bath off the hallway and began brushing her teeth.

Grady slid off his shoes and walked to the doorway she had left ajar. He looked in as she was spitting in the sink, one hand pressed against her chest to keep her necklace from swinging into the spray, the other hand holding her wet hair back in a loose knot. "Excuse me," she said, as she reached for the hand towel hanging on the wall next to where he stood.

"Can you talk for a second?" he asked.

"Look, Grady. I've got to go. What is it?"

"Since the summer I've been trying to make sense of things," he said, holding up the crinkled envelope thick with his prose. "I told you some of this already the night I came over for dinner. I'm not trying to make excuses—I just want you to know the whole story."

"So what? Is this your memoir or something? Let me guess. I'll read it, and suddenly you and the other night in your apartment and the fist fight in the parking lot and the phone call from jail—all of it will make perfect sense, right?"

"You have a right to be angry, Susan," he said, as he followed her out into the hallway. "I haven't been totally honest with you, and you've been nothing but kind to me."

She stepped toward him and grabbed his shoulders lightly. "This is all very fascinating, really it is, but I have to go to work." She brushed past him toward the door.

"Can you wait?" he asked.

But she grabbed her keys off the front table and turned toward him. "Whatever you've got for me, just leave it there on the table. I'll attend to it when I can."

"Thanks," he said. "I grabbed your paper too, but you might want to read what's in the envelope before you read the front page."

"I can only imagine," she said, shaking her head as she took the newspaper out of his hand. "Close the door when you're done here, okay?"

"I'm done," he said, but she was already walking to her car.

On the way home, Grady stopped at the store to purchase some food and a copy of the newspaper for himself. He spent the rest of the morning and most of the afternoon reading every article except the one beginning under his picture on the front page. He made an early dinner and sat down to eat it before he finally gave in and read the account of the incident at the gallery. When he finished, he cleaned his dishes and pulled the smoke alarm down from the kitchen ceiling. Then he stood next to the sink and, holding the long sheets high over the stainless steel basin, burned each page on which his name appeared. His face was void of expression as the paper turned to ash before him.

The phone rang at 9:00 p.m.

"Grady, it's Susan."

"I didn't know if you'd call."

"I just finished reading your work."

"You're a fast reader."

"I came home on my lunch hour and picked it up. I've been reading it all afternoon." He didn't know what to say. "Are you around? Can we talk in person?" she asked.

"Yeah, I mean, that's what I was hoping for. Where are you?"

"I'm at the apartment," she said. "But my mom's sleeping. Why don't we meet at my place in Apollo. That way we can talk without worrying about disturbing her."

"Okay, Susan, I'll be over."

"Give me about a half an hour," she said, and hung up the phone.

She was waiting on the top step of the porch when he got there. The light of the house glowed softly behind her. She had changed out of her work clothes and looked relaxed in a pair of jeans and a heavy cotton sweater.

"Hey," he said, as he made his way up the walk. "Thanks for calling, I didn't know if …"

"I'm sorry for how I acted earlier today," she said, interrupting. "I was angry, maybe even a little hurt. But I've got the house warmed up, and I've opened a nice bottle of cabernet. We could go inside if you want."

Grady felt the chill of night air and looked at Susan standing before him framed in the light of her home. "Do you want to walk a while?" he said. Without saying another word, she turned up the porch and locked the door. Then she walked down the steps, and they headed off together down the streets of Apollo.

They walked through the town, circling blocks as the night settled in over them. They followed the sidewalk past the Red Newt Art Gallery, past his parents' house with the lights turned out in the cold, until at last they found themselves standing in the dewy grass on the brink of the vast and broken field where Worthingdale Woods once stood.

"I guess I hadn't realized that all of this would happen so quickly," Grady said pointing to the expanse of upturned soil in the distance.

"The paper said they wanted to get the lots timbered before the heavy snows."

Grady took a step back, as if to leave and said, "So much of my life happened here, and now there's just... nothing."

Susan was silent for a beat. Then turning to face him, she asked, "What happened after Emile found you in the woods, Grady?"

He winced and let out a sharp breath then looked away from her into the darkness. "That's a fair question," he said. "You deserve to know what you're getting into." Her only response was to take his hand.

"My grandfather was a Marine in World War II. When he heard we joined the Boy Scouts, he gave his old Ka-Bar knife to Emile. My parents took it away of course, but Emile knew where they kept it. He had it with him that day.

"You wrote that he had blood on him."

"He blamed me for what happened. He said, if I had kept my word and shown up to fight in the water war, the fawn never would have died. I shouted back at him, but he fell on me. I fought him off the best I could, but he was older and stronger. It was over quickly, but I was pretty beat up."

"So why did he stop?"

"See, we ended up next to the fawn's body; almost on top of it. Emile was holding my face to the ground. Shouting at me to look at what I had done. That's when I noticed it was still breathing."

"The fawn wasn't dead?"

"It seemed dead. But when I was lying there, with my face right up against it, I felt its breath. Emile stopped when I screamed. He could tell something was wrong."

"What did he do? I mean, what happened then?"

"He started talking in this very high pitched, hysterical voice—hugging the fawn's head and begging for forgiveness. Then, he pulled out the knife and told me I had to 'finish what I started'—that's how he put it.

"It was probably mostly in my head, but I remember feeling terribly threatened. It's not like Emile would have killed me. But anyway, I felt like I didn't have a choice."

"But if it was almost dead... I mean I'm not a hunter, but wouldn't it have been rather simple to... finish it?" Susan flinched around the last of her words.

Grady nodded. "Yes. But that's not what happened."

"What do you mean?"

"This feeling I can't really explain came over me. I just wanted to destroy it. To kill it good and dead. It was like I was a wild animal. I went berserk. I can still hear the sound of its ribs breaking. I was covered in blood and fur." Grady looked at his arms as if the stain was still there. "There wasn't much left of the body when I finally stopped.

"You have to understand the circumstances, Susan. It was so hot. I was afraid. Terrified really. My head felt swollen. It was hard to think, you know?" Susan gazed back with a mixture of terror and sadness in her eyes.

"You've never seen so much blood. The ground was thick with it. It took me days to get it out from under my fingernails."

"I can't believe Emile didn't try to stop you," she said. "Maybe he was afraid.

"Yeah, either that or something else."

"What do you mean, something else?"

"Well, the expression on Emile's face when I finally looked up." Grady's voice dropped to an awed whisper. "That's the thing that haunts me the most about that afternoon."

"What?"

"He was smiling, Susan"

"Smiling?"

"His eyes were almost shining. And there was dirt on his teeth. I'll never forget that dirt."

"Did he say anything to you?"

Nothing Here is Real

"He might have, I can't really remember, because when I saw that look on his face, I just ran away as fast as I could. I swear."

"Did Emile follow you?"

"I never looked back. I went to the creek and washed off the best I could. It was probably an hour before I made it home again. Emile was already there when I got back. Like nothing had happened. No one even asked me where I was."

"Unbelievable."

"You know, it's weird, Susan. It's like sometimes I think this is the one place on earth that knows me best. If a place can know a person."

"Why's that?" Susan asked.

"It's where all my evil and goodness come together."

"What goodness?" she asked.

"Remember how I told you about the ashes. That box Briarly gave me?"

"Yes."

"That's the first thing I did when I came back to town. I came here and spread those ashes in the woods."

"What? Why, Grady?"

"I wanted to make things right, Susan. To make amends for what I did—for who I was in that moment." Grady was far away from her now. "But now, this place is just nothing. Clelland's houses. And I just can't help feeling like I've betrayed my daughter in some deep and unforgivable way."

"The woods may be gone," Susan spoke sternly, "but if I have any say in it, Clelland won't have his hands on this land for long."

"What do you mean?" Grady asked, pulling himself together.

"Remember how I told you about Veteran Renewal pumping asbestos insulation into all those houses in Eden Heights?"

"Yeah, but you said none of the accusations would stick to Keith because he'd joined the business after he got back from the war."

"That's what we thought, but it turns out he's been either too cocky or too dumb to stop doing it. My firm's got a paper trail that proves he's got plans to do the same thing with the houses he's going to build here at the Glenwoods Development."

"Does he know you guys know about this?"

"He will tomorrow, when he's presented with the court injunction to stop all construction activity until the evidence plays itself out in court."

"But how can he be held accountable for a crime he hasn't committed yet? You only have evidence of his plan to build illegally here."

"You're right. We can't really bust him for what he's yet to do, but with the evidence we have, we've got a good chance of connecting the dots back to the houses in Eden Heights. Best case scenario, he goes to jail; worse case, at least he loses this contract. I'm not a betting woman, but if I were, I'd say there won't be a development here anytime soon. Your daughter's ashes are safe."

Slowly she reached down and took hold of his thumb. His fingers curled around hers. "You've got to believe you won't always feel like this," she said. He nodded but didn't speak. After a moment, she turned them away from the field, and he followed her through the streets of the town he had always called home.

It was late by the time they returned to her house. As they walked the final blocks, Susan convinced him to stay the night. For one night anyway, he could sleep without fear of ghosts.

He watched silently as she lay out a bed for him on the couch. When he lay down on the sheets, she bent over him and gently kissed his forehead. Grady followed her with his eyes as she turned to go upstairs to sleep. When her shadow crossed through the glow of the streetlight pouring through the living room window, he stood to stop her.

"Susan?"

"What is it?" she asked. His silence was a plea.

For a moment she was still. Then she walked toward him. When she took him in her arms, he began to weep against her shoulder.

She rose to touch her lips to his. Her hands moved gracefully over his body, peeling him free of his clothes. She lay a blanket on the ground. In the cold of the room, he lay back on it, naked and hard before her. She pulled her shirt over her head. Then rubbing her hands down her hips, she locked her thumbs on the waist of her pants. As she bent to pull them down to the ground, her breasts swung free before him. He looked into her eyes again as she rose to step out of the last of her clothes. For a moment she stood, dipped in light, then she slowly lowered herself down onto him. He felt the heat of her skin against the cold, the softness of her lips on his chin. She turned her face away and gulped a breath as he slid himself fully inside her. His mouth next to her ear said her name over and over again as their bodies moved together in the night.

After some time his breath grew short. She half lifted herself off him and began to sway on top of his body, her hips rising and falling in time. His hands kneaded and pulled her toward him. Her hair fell across his face and chest.

In a fury now, their bodies loved one another. His arms pulled her fully on top of him, and she cried out, shuddering against the moment of release. She gasped with the force of his final movements, letting her body collapse, wholly spent.

They lay for a long time, silent, naked and panting. Grady was the first to speak. "You can't know what that means to me."

She sighed and rubbed her right hand down his chest and past his stomach. With her left hand she reached over and gently held him soft against her. "I've never known what that's felt like," she whispered. "To have it be like that."

After a while he pulled the blanket over them, and soon they were both asleep. Sometime in the night she roused him, and together they made their way up to the bed. They slept soundly holding each other.

Grady woke in the cool of the morning. Susan was gone. The house was silent. He found his clothes folded neatly on the coffee table at the end of the bed. When he went downstairs, he saw that the couch was pushed back into place. The blanket, pillow, and sheet she had used to make up the bed the night before were nowhere to be seen.

He walked into the kitchen. On the refrigerator he found her note inviting him to stay.

He went upstairs and showered. When he came back down, he made himself breakfast and stood in the kitchen, eating his cereal. Overnight, a dusting of snow had gathered, and in the morning light, it appeared as though it was going to stick. He stood in the kitchen re-reading the note Susan had left for him. He flipped it over and found a pen. His words assured her that after he gathered a few things from his place, he would come back to stay.

3.

He drove the sedan in four long, lazy laps around town before pulling up to the front of the building that housed Ward Gregory's old apartment. Once he was upstairs, he packed a duffle bag with some clothes, his running shoes, his toothbrush, and a razor. His eyes scanned the modest kitchen: the clock, the filthy stove, the black refrigerator, the empty chair where Susan had sat, the small wood table with the phone and address book on it. His eyes stopped there. The phone was blinking. Someone must have called when he was at Susan's the night before. He walked over to the answering machine, and pushed the play button.

> *Grady, this is your mother calling…I know you're not at work. Pick up the phone! …Fine, if you want to play this game, I'll just say what I have to say on tape. Do you know what you've done to this family? Your father goes down to the police station to bail you out of jail, and you end up screaming at him? It's bad enough that you nearly killed your brother, but to ignore Emile's calls after he, in Christian charity, decides to forgive you and drop the charges*

*in the hope of bringing you to the light of Christ.
And by the way, your little charade is up—Emile
told us everything last night. I just don't know if I'll
ever be able to trust you again. I'd come over there,
but frankly I don't think it's safe. Then again, maybe
you're not there. Maybe you're at that woman Susan
Luster's house. Do you know she had the audacity to
call this house? God, tell me that's not true...when
people ask me, I want to deny it, but I honestly don't
know anymore. I honestly don't know. At any rate,
this is your mother—you remember, I'm sure: the
woman who raised you. I suggest, if you'd still like
to consider yourself part of this family, you call this
house the second you get this message.*

When the last echo of his mother's voice faded
from the room he pushed his finger down on the delete
button. He stood for a moment looking down at the once-
blinking light, his fists clenched at his sides. "Fine, bitch,"
he said. Then he grabbed his coat out of his bedroom
closet, and let the apartment door slam behind him.

When Grady, in a blind rage, threw open the door
to his parents' house, he was greeted by the broken visage

of his brother staring back at him from the other side of the threshold. Emile's entire face was swollen and covered in lacerations. Sixteen stitches traced a puffy arch of pink skin above his eye. Grady took a stunned step back. Seeing his brother falter, Emile said sharply, "You've got a lot of nerve walking in this house. What are you doing here?"

"Get the fuck out of my way, Emile," Grady said, gathering himself. "I'm here to talk to Mom."

"I asked you a question," Emile answered, his Adam's apple bobbing on his neck. "Are you alone?"

"What does that mean, 'Am I alone?'"

"I didn't know if your lawyer friend was with you."

"Look, Emile," he said, ignoring the bait, "Mom called, and I came here when I got the message."

"That's quite a bruise," Emile said. "It looks like they did a good job with the stitches, though. That probably won't leave too much of a scar."

Grady nodded. "Doesn't look like you'll be quite as lucky. Now get out of my way."

"Or else what? Are you going to try to fight me again? That turned out so well for you the last time." Emile smiled coyly as he spoke.

Pausing and settling on his feet, Grady said, "As far as I can see, Emile, there aren't any crazy people to blindside me with a sign, or get in a cheap shot while I'm down, so I recommend you step aside, unless you're hoping to get hurt."

"Mom's not here. She called and asked that I come and watch the house while she was gone."

"'Watch the house?' What does that mean?"

"It means she's afraid of you, Grady. Afraid of what you might do."

Grady wordlessly turned to leave.

"Heading off to Susan's to lick your wounds are you? Or is it back to Ward Gregory's old place?" Grady ignored him as he walked toward the car. "You can't run from the truth of your life, Grady. Eventually, your sins will catch up to you." Emile called after him.

Grady spun around to face his brother. "I've got nothing to hide from, Emile. Can you say the same thing?"

"I've confessed myself to God."

"And tell me, Emile, was the priest who heard your confession the same one who put you up to all this Coalition bullshit, or is this just your fucked up way of trying to make amends for your past?"

"I'm not the one who has to worry about the past. I've been forgiven. Can you say the same?"

"I've got nothing to ask forgiveness for," Grady said firmly.

"I wonder if your daughter would agree?"

Nothing Here is Real

Grady recoiled as if struck by a blow. "Where does this hate come from, Emile?"

"I don't hate you, I hate what you've done."

"Not me. I haven't done anything worthy of that comment and you know it. What is it you hate so much about yourself that you have to hide behind this veil of lies?"

"How lyrical." Emile cleared his throat. "Let me tell you something, Grady, you don't know anything about me, okay. You never have."

"Are you happy, Emile?"

"I'm right," he said. "That's enough for me."

"But are you happy? I mean, does all of this hating in the name of God make you feel better about who you are?"

"You have no idea who I am. No idea what it's been like for me . . ."

"You know Emile, sometimes, I think Ward Gregory was right: if you can see the truth of your own life, what does it matter if everyone else can only sees lies?" And then he was gone.

4.

Susan was in the kitchen, hovering over some pots on the stove when Grady came in. He walked up behind her and gently squeezed her hips. "How was work?"

She raised a glass of wine and said, "I've opened some wine, and there's some beer in the fridge."

"So you're either drowning your sorrows or toasting your success."

"Drowning your sorrows is so cliché," she smiled.

"So it's a victory, then?" he asked.

"I don't want to jinx things, but it looks good."

"He's going to jail?"

"That remains to be seen and probably won't be settled for a long time, but I can confidently say the woods, or what's left of them, aren't in his hands anymore."

He took his coat off and threw it on the back of a chair. "That's awesome news."

She took another drink. "How about you? Did you get what you went back to your apartment for?"

"Yeah, I did, after all of that."

"After all of what?"

"I've had a crazy afternoon," he said, helping

himself to a beer. "My mother left a bitchy message on my machine, so I went over to the house to talk to her, but Emile was there instead."

"What?"

"Yeah, according to Emile, she'd left him to guard the house in case I came while she was gone."

"Do you really think she said that?"

"It's just more of his bullshit, Susan. He's been lying to himself for so long I don't think he even knows what's true anymore. What's even better is I'm pretty sure he's got my mother believing that I convinced Briarly to have an abortion."

"What? Why would he ever say something like that, and why would your parents ever believe him?"

Grady took a long, thoughtful swig of beer. "I think Ward Gregory's death taught Emile that if you tell yourself a lie enough times, it starts to look like the truth, and eventually you can use it to suit your needs."

"What does Ward Gregory have to do with what happened to your daughter?"

"The more I think about it, the more I'm thinking that maybe there was something going on between Emile and Ward Gregory—something on an emotional level that Emile was ashamed of. I think he came close to telling me about it in his bedroom, but changed the story at the last second instead. When I called his bluff and made him tell my parents about supposedly being abused, Emile had to find a way to make the whole thing go away. You remember the phone cord I saw leading to Emile's room? My bet is after he told my parents, he took the phone into his room and called Gregory."

"And told him what?"

Grady shrugged and said, "Maybe Emile told him why my mother was on her way over, and Gregory saw death as the only way out of the mess my brother created for him. If you think about it, it makes sense. I don't know, but whatever Emile said, it was something that made the guy kill himself." He downed the last of his beer.

"You're saying your brother wanted Ward Gregory dead?"

"No, but I do think Ward Gregory's death saved Emile a lot of explaining."

"I guess that could be true," Susan offered, "but none of this explains why he wants your parents to believe you and Briarly got an abortion."

"In a way it's kind of the same thing," Grady explained. "Emile has to make sure the real truth about his past will never get out, especially with the Vita Coalition pulling stunts at local abortion clinics. If he convinces everybody that Briarly got an abortion, nobody would ever believe me if I decided to tell them the truth about what happened when Emile was away at college.

"See, Emile lives his life as if he's always being accused of doing something wrong, and for some reason, he sees me as his number one accuser. I think he believes if he can somehow convince the world I'm a bad person, then what I think of him won't matter."

"Grady, as a lawyer, I've got to tell you, you sound pretty paranoid. I don't doubt that Emile is deeply disturbed, but why would he, all of a sudden, start making up these lies about you when it was years and years ago that he confessed to this affair with the college girl? I mean, if he was worried about you betraying him, why wouldn't he have tried to discredit you earlier?"

"Think about what would happen to the Vita Coalition if word got out that Emile had a sexual encounter in college that resulted in an abortion. He's got to cover his tracks. This is the only way to do it. The facts don't matter. If other people believe Emile's lies, the damage is already done."

She stood before him, her arms folded across her chest, shaking her head in disbelief. "So what are you going to do now?"

"What do you mean?"

"I mean, about your job, living here, everything."

"I don't really know," he admitted.

"Well, do you want to know what I think?"

"You read my mind."

"I think the only way you'll be free of all this, Grady, is if you find a way to let go of who you want them to be. Everyone's family is screwed up. I mean, do you honestly think I enjoy taking care of my mother? Besides," she said, running her hand down his chest, "I don't want you to leave."

"That's quite a closing argument, counselor."

"Screw you," she laughed. "I'm serious."

"I know you are, Susan, but..." Before he could continue, she put her hand on his shoulder.

"Grady, I know this thing between us is new. I don't want to rush anything, but last night felt real to me, you know?" Grady turned and looked at her. "I guess what I'm saying is, I'm willing to try things out. To give it a shot."

"Me too, but what does that have to do with anything we're talking about now?" he asked.

"Love is risky. Sometimes you just have to have faith things will work out as they're supposed to."

"Are we talking about my family now or are we talking about us?"

"Both. Kind of," she said.

"What are you trying to say?"

Nothing Here is Real

"You could stay with me," she said. "You know, move in."

Grady took a step away from her and leaned against the counter. "What about your mom?" he asked.

"My mom is happy enough sitting in her chair listening to the police scanner all day. Anyway, she's eighty-six, and she's got diabetes. The long term prognosis isn't great."

"I don't know," he said. "I can't live off your charity forever, Susan. You've already given me too much I can't repay."

"Did last night feel like charity to you?" she asked.

"No, it's just . . ." Frustrated, he turned away. "That was just one night." As soon as the words were out of his mouth, he could tell he hurt her.

"It didn't feel that way to me," she said, as she walked briskly out of the room.

"Susan, wait." He followed after her, but she was already walking toward the stairs. When he heard her bedroom door close behind her, he stood at the bottom of the stairs for a few minutes waiting for her to change her mind. When she didn't return, he grabbed his coat, bag, and laptop and walked out of the house alone.

5.

Grady drove across town and, after parking behind the building, climbed the stairs to Ward Gregory's old apartment. He didn't turn on any lights or stop in the kitchen to check his messages, but instead walked straight to the bedroom and began taking off his clothes. Despite the cold, he cracked open the window and climbed into bed. He lay on his back, feeling the cold air rush over his body.

At once he was struck by the memory of the room that was to be the nursery. One day, while Briarly was away at a conference, he painted the molding the wrong color. When she came home, they fought about it. He left to go for a run to blow off some steam. She went to the store and bought a new bucket of paint. When he came home she was quietly painting over the color that caused their argument. Covered in sweat, he picked up a brush and joined her in finishing the room. Then he took her to their bed and made love to her. It was the last time before the baby died. The last time before Susan.

Grady got out of bed and pushed the window shut. Then he sat back down and pulled out his phone. He let his fingers push her number without knowing for sure what he'd say. Her recorded voice broke the silence. Did he really expect she would pick up?

After a pause he spoke to her as if she were there: "You asked me why all of this had to happen. That's the last thing you said to me. So I came back to Apollo, to try to make sense of it. I mean, to try to understand if what happened to us was because of me—because of the things I did, the secrets I've kept, the person I am capable of being. But everything is messed up now, Briarly. And I don't know the answer. I don't know where else to look. I guess I'll leave it up to you to show me the way." But as he hung up, he felt certain she was gone, and with her the person he was before the clinic. He turned off his phone.

His eyes fell on the half-packed duffle bag sitting on the floor. When he found his running shoes, he tossed them on the bed. He dug out a pair of sweats and a knit hat to wear against the cold. Then he tied the shoes onto his feet. Without turning on a light, he left the apartment behind and headed down the streets of Apollo, toward the field where the woods once stood.

He felt the dampness of the grass soak into his shoes as he made his way across the schoolyard. The dusting of snow that had gathered a few days before was only on the edges of the world now. In the darkness, it looked as though the upturned earth before him was coated with a feather shake of powdered sugar clinging to the ridges of the displaced soil. As he came to the threshold of grass and earth, he stopped to survey the deeply rutted ground.

It was as silent as a tomb. The heavy clouds hanging in the sky stifled the light of the stars. He turned away from where the woods once stood and ran toward the creek instead.

He approached the head of the bike trail that ran along the bank of the Shenengo and slowed to a near-walk. The trail was wide enough for a small car and offered even footing. Grady pounded forward in near blindness. His eyes sought any available light, but there was nothing to guide his way save the sound of the creek on his right and the occasional snap of the gravel beneath his shoes. The dense branches on either side of the trail gave Grady the haunting impression of being inside the darkened tunnel that ran under Water Street, depositing itself behind the graveyard where the people of Apollo buried their dead.

He wasn't sure how long he had been running when he saw a hole of light burrowing out of the darkness ahead of him. As he ran forward, he recognized the lantern that stood by the West Street entrance to the trail. His clothes were drenched in sweat and a fine steam of his body's heat mixing with the creeping cold of the night surrounded him as he hurled his body toward its goal.

He was lost in the struggle to reach the end of the trail, focused only on the light shining before him, when two deer broke noiselessly through the hedges. Out of his singular focus, he shouted, jumped, and stopped running—startled into a new and full consciousness. For the first instant it seemed as though the doe and her fawn were running in stride with him, but his loud cry caused them to burst forward with new energy, their legs a blur in the night. With their white trails high, the creatures broke into the light of the lantern.

Turning back into the darkness, they stood panting in the cold, their ears alert, their eyes mirrors of the night. Slowly Grady began to walk forward toward the deer, sure something in their being beseeched him to follow.

Suddenly, as if yanked by a string, the heads of the doe and her fawn jerked sideways and their bodies followed out of sight. Desperate to see them, even as they disappeared, Grady broke into a full sprint, his body slicing out of the darkness of the trail, and into the lights of Apollo. For a moment, he stopped in the lantern's spotlight, a heaving mass of humanity, his eyes searching desperately for the deer. Then he found them together in the shadows. They stood on the cusp of the bank. The creek ran freely behind them.

He did not turn to see the truck coming toward him, but its lights flashed in their eyes, as the angry revving of its engine screamed into the night. In the last instant, he felt comfort in knowing that at least they were together as their bodies disappeared into the darkness. Together they begged him to follow.

The doe and fawn disappeared over the edge as one body. Somehow Grady was carried with them. The truck followed at full acceleration, snapping off the lamppost as it went. Grady saw the headlights twisting and jumping as the truck rolled toward the creek. The sharp smell of gasoline filled his nose as he pinwheeled down the bank. He heard the crush of metal against wood and stone. With his eyes closed to the violent swirl of the fall, he felt himself rising above his body. At a distance, he saw himself crash again and again against the freshly ravaged earth. He did not feel the sting of pain, but only the palpable sensation of being pulled away from the carnage.

Near the bottom of the bank, his body still tossing through the air, his right thigh caught the edge of a half-fallen tree. The force of bone and muscle against wood wrapped his torso forward and his head crashed to the earth, his arms splayed out before him. At last he was still.

Then it was as if he were looking down at his broken body from a great height. Seeing it there, bent at the waist and contorted unnaturally against the damp trunk of the tree, he felt a sudden cold breath ease through his body. For a moment he was sure that pain would never come again. But just as quickly his ears were full of the sound of water against rocks. Then blackness.

When he got to the edge of the creek he saw the crushed truck tossed on its driver's side in a deep pool amidst the rising, rollicking water. Somehow its lone exposed headlight had remained intact and now cast a broken beam upstream.

Grady was already waist deep in the water, unconsciously moving toward the truck when his body first convulsed against the cold. His breath was gone by the time he reached the wreckage. He clung to the riding board and pulled himself up out of the water. He tried the door, but he had no leverage to lift it. Bracing his right foot against the front passenger wheel well and rising as best he could on the slick surface of the truck side, he pulled again at the door handle, but it slipped coldly from his grasp. His hand was thrust against his chest in a counterpunch of failed effort that knocked him back into the water.

Fighting against the current, Grady again shimmied up the passenger-side door and looked, through the wave-splashed window, into the truck's cab. He found himself inches away from the blood-smeared face of a desperate boy.

The cab of the truck was almost full of water. Somewhere beneath the boy, Grady could make out the crushed shoulder and twisted arm of the driver. The boy's hands were pressed against the glass, and his eyes rolled with fright.

Without thinking Grady raised his fist high into the air and brought it crashing down against the passenger side window. There was already blood when he pulled it back through the broken glass. When his fist fell again there was space enough for him to reach in and grab hold of the boy's face. Grady pulled the head through the ragged hole and into the night air.

At first there was so much blood it was hard to see if the boy was still alive, but then a fresh wave spilled over the truck, and the boy began to cry and gasp. Grady shouted, "Help will come. I'll stay here with you." The boy did not answer, but Grady could hear his cries above the flow of the raging water, as if he had been listening for them all of his life.

6.

When she heard the door close behind Grady, she allowed herself some time to cry over "Just one night." But she had spent too many nights alone in her life to wallow in self-pity over him. She went downstairs, wrapped up the dinner she made for the two of them, and drove over to her mother's apartment.

Janet Luster sat in her chair, fading in and out of sleep, the warmed up meal on her lap, the police scanner droning on in the background. Susan was telling her about seeing Grady at the meeting, the night at The Well, the sweet kiss at her place, and how he'd shown up the morning after he got out of jail. She stopped short of telling her about the sex but thought she might, just to see if sharing such intimate details could stir her mother into an awareness of how desperate Susan felt.

Her mother's only reply was to scratch her nose and turn around in her chair to tweak the setting of the scanner. After listening to the static for a minute, she said, "He sounds like trouble to me, Suzie girl."

"Isn't that what you always say about men, mother?"

"Isn't it always true?" she replied.

Susan got up and took her covered dish to the kitchen. When she came back into the room, she found her mother turned toward the scanner again. "Mother, if you're going to tinker with that thing all night, I might as well go home."

"Hush up, will you!" she chided. "There's been a car accident in Apollo. Sounds like three people might be dead. They got the jaws of life there and everything."

Susan's heart knew right away. "Did they say which hospital they're taking them to, Mom?"

"Oh, all of a sudden the scanner's not such a silly little toy, huh?"

"Tell me the goddamn hospital, Mother!" she shouted.

"General, I think," her mother responded. "What's all the yelling about?" But Susan was out the door before her mother finished talking.

Susan burst through the emergency room door screaming Grady's name. The nurse behind the counter didn't ask any questions, but instead wordlessly led Susan into a small consultation room. "Someone will be in to see you shortly," she said.

A bearded doctor opened the door a minute later.

Nothing Here is Real

"Mrs. Pickett?" the doctor asked, and Susan said yes. The doctor gently shook her hand and sat down in the plastic chair across from her. "Before he lost consciousness, your husband was asking about you."

"What's going on? Will he be alright?"

"Your husband was involved in a terrible accident. He has multiple compound fractures in his right hand and several veins were severed on his right wrist. These injuries have caused him to lose a great deal of blood. At first we couldn't stop the bleeding. We've done a transfusion. He's also punctured a lung. That's the bad news. The good news is, he's alive."

"Oh, thank God," she said. "Thank God." She breathed deeply in front of the doctor, as he waited for her to compose herself. After a minute she looked up and asked, "How did all of this happen?" The doctor turned and knocked on the shut door. A state trooper opened it. The doctor nodded at him without speaking, looked back at Susan, and walked out of the room.

The trooper explained how when he arrived on the scene of the accident, he found the lantern's post sheered clean off the ground. The small trees and shrubs on the other side of the sidewalk next to the steep creek bank were all torn from their roots as well. The trooper followed the wreckage down the bank and saw the red pickup crushed upside down in the creek's high running water.

"I don't understand," Susan said. "Was Grady in the truck?"

"Mrs. Pickett," the trooper said. "From what I can gather your husband was out for a run near the bike path. The truck was going too fast around the corner where the trail ends and meets up with the sidewalk. The driver must have lost control of the vehicle, because there weren't any skid marks to speak of. Anyway, the truck plowed right through the post and was going at such a speed it continued down the embankment and into the Shenengo Creek. Judging from the damage, it probably flipped over a few times before it settled in the water."

"But Grady wasn't hit?"

"No, he'd be dead for sure."

"But I don't understand then, officer. How is it that he's injured if the truck didn't hit him?"

"He must have somehow jumped out of the way. Another few seconds here or there and he'd have died for sure.

"When I got down to the water, your husband was punching out the windows of the truck. He busted up his hand and sliced up his wrist, but he got the boy's head out enough to breathe. We tried to get to the father, but the cab was too crushed. We needed the jaws of life just to get to the body."

Later when Susan was asked to show identification, so she might help the trooper fill out some paperwork, it was revealed she was not "Mrs. Pickett." She was scolded and escorted back to the general waiting room where she resolved to sleep out the night, hoping one of the nurses would find the kindness to update her on Grady's condition. Susan sat alone watching the endless cycles of information spewing from the local 24-hour cable-access news station. She could think of nothing else to do.

At 2:00 in the morning, a fresh cycle of the broadcast revealed there had been a one-vehicle accident earlier that evening in Apollo. The driver was killed. The passenger, his son, remained in critical condition in the hospital. A third man, who attempted a rescue at the scene, was also in the hospital with severe injuries.

An hour later the same station led with the story of the accident in Apollo because they now knew the drunk driver was the decorated war veteran Keith Clelland. Though his father was dead, the son's condition had been upgraded from critical to serious.

The news also reported the identity of the man who was injured on the scene while attempting to rescue Clelland and his boy from the icy waters of the creek.

"Grady Pickett, of Apollo," the reporter said. Then, to be clear, he added, "The high school teacher recently involved in an assault scandal at a local art gallery." She was alone in the waiting room, so Susan got up and shut off the television. She sat back down in the chair and closed her eyes, waiting to be embraced by the silence of sleep.

THANKSGIVING

Thanksgiving night, after the turkey was finished, the games were over, and Grady had driven Susan's mother back to the apartment, he told Susan he needed to go for a walk to clear his head. He kissed her gently and promised to be home before it got too late.

He walked around the quiet streets of Apollo, looking in the windows at the families playing out their lives in pantomime before him. His head and stomach felt heavy from the turkey and wine of dinner, but in the crisp night air he felt stirred to continue.

A week after Grady came home from the hospital, Keith Clelland was buried in the Chestnut Street Cemetery with full military honors. Seamus remained in serious condition with severe head trauma and several broken bones. He was unable to attend his father's funeral.

Susan drove Grady home after he was released from the hospital. To be fair to the landlord, he promised to continue to pay rent on Ward Gregory's apartment through the first of the year, but he swore to Susan he would never sleep there again.

Nothing Here is Real

Grady resigned his teaching position at Eden Heights. He would clean out his things once he regained full use of his hand. It was better for everyone that way, he explained.

After ignoring several of their calls, Grady finally had gotten back to his parents late one night. They both got on the line. They didn't ask many questions, and seemed pleased to hear his voice. He told them about moving in with Susan. He told them things were good; he was happy. Then he got off the phone.

His mother called the Monday before Thanksgiving, inviting Grady and Susan to join them for the meal. She told him she was trying to be nice. She said she wanted to make things right again. Grady said he wanted that too, but that they had already made their plans.

All of November flickered through his mind as he walked across town. He didn't stop until he rounded the corner of Gendel Street. There Grady stood in the shadows of Ward Gregory's lot looking in on his family finishing their Thanksgiving meal. His father was serving warm pumpkin pie onto plates of good china that were only used twice a year. His mother stood next to Frank with a heavy ice cream scoop in her hand, a tub of French vanilla open before her. Sarah was carrying away the dinner dishes.

Emile sat with his hands in his lap, waiting to be served.

Grady stepped back to survey the house from a distance. How small it seemed from where he stood. The fenced-in yard, the washed brick driveway, the garage with its tools all hung in their place. All of it seemed somehow separate, as if his life there had existed only as a broken fragment of a dream from some long ago, forgotten time.

As he began to leave, he saw his mother laughing and remembered when, as a young child, he had come home from school and found the baby robin he had rescued from a fallen nest, dead in the bottom of the shoebox where he had been keeping it. He went to his mother and clung to the side of her white sweater until it was wet with his tears. She stroked his hair and held him in her lap. When at last he looked up at her, she was smiling down on him, her lips pursed open in a soft and gentle song. At once he had felt the warmth of being loved beyond question.

Looking in through the window, Grady thought if time was a thing that could be broken and pieced together again without the shards of loss, or if there was a way to shine back through the past and spill the love gathered there out over the path of days that were to come, surely he would do that for the empty shadows that moved before him now, so they might somehow find some peace.

Nothing Here is Real

It was late now, and he was tired. Still, as he turned away he began to run, purposefully picking up speed as the streets leading to Susan's faded into the distance, and the field where he had scattered the ashes came into view.

With the town at last behind him, he stopped and stood alone on the brink of the outer darkness. The shortness of his breath made his lungs feel wet inside his body. His hand throbbed painfully. The wind blew across the empty furrows and rose through the treeless expanse. The chill of the night threatened to take hold of his being. Then he tilted his head upward and saw the broad freedom of the sky laid bare before him.

Some men claim their life is drawn in the book of time before their first earthly breath meets the air of this world. Others swear they are caught in a web of choice and circumstance. With his eyes closed to the night, Grady could still clearly see the lines of the stars, for theirs is a light that burns long beyond extinction.

He crossed over the threshold of the upturned earth and faced the night's sweet, untethered wind. As he pushed forward into the darkness, he felt certain he could run forever.

Acknowledgments

My gratitude runs deep to the many who have helped me along the way. I am specifically grateful for Luke Gutelius and Kim Philips who read early drafts of this book with sincerity born out of friendship. And for Matt Sawyer, Mike Spillman, and Niki Gernold whose candor and encouragement refreshed me. And also for Diane Bond and Mark and Amy Vanderwater, who divinely swept into my life at just the right time.

Thanks to Paul Frederick, whose red pen and infinite patience sharpened my words. And to Emily Tomasik and Mark McCune, artists in their own right, who read with fresh eyes the story of their old teacher.

A special debt of gratitude is owed to Rick Ohler, Mick Cochrane and Gary Earl Ross who unselfishly gave their time and perspective. And to my extraordinary editor, Andria Cole, whose skillful eye, dedicated hand, and open heart made nearly every page of this novel better.

I am deeply indebted to Mary Patroulis, who challenged me to tell the story that mattered most, Ami Ford-Cammarota, who gave me courage in the face of doubt, and Kristen Farrell, who willingly gave this story her whole heart.

Thanks also to my mother, father and brother. So much of this is owed to the three of you. You gave me what all writers yearn for: lots of material. But also lots of love. Thanks for that. And the same goes for my students.

But I save my largest thanks for my wife, Theresa, who loves all the imperfect parts of me. Thank you for giving me the time and space to tell the story I needed to tell, and for your relentless belief in me.

About the Author

Matt Bindig was raised outside of Buffalo, New York. He was educated at Hobart College and Harvard University. He lives with his wife and children in the Buffalo area where he teaches high school English. *Nothing Here is Real* is his first novel.

CPSIA information can be obtained at www.ICGtesting.com
Printed in the USA
BVOW08s0722150516

448139BV00001B/5/P